APPLEGATE LANDING

Jean Conrad

Serenade/Saga
BOOKS
of the Zondervan Publishing House
Grand Rapids, Michigan

Applegate Landing
Copyright © 1985 by The Zondervan Corporation
Grand Rapids, Michigan

Serenade/Saga is an imprint of Zondervan Publishing House,
1415 Lake Drive, S.E., Grand Rapids, Michigan 49506.

ISBN 0-310-46832-9

Edited by Nancye Willis
Designed by Kim Koning

Printed in the United States of America

85 86 87 88 89 90 91 / 10 9 8 7 6 5 4 3 2 1

For my mother, Bonnie Conrad,
whose memories of southern Oregon
and whose missionary grandparents
inspired this story

CHAPTER 1

GRAY WISPS OF OCEAN FOG curled around massive redwood trunks, deepening the quiet gloom of the primeval forest. From her rough seat on a mule-drawn freight wagon, lurching slowly along a rutted path through the trees, Gloriana Windemere peered into the shadows, trying not to imagine savage, dark faces peering back at her. Overhead in the treetops, sunlight filtered through the branches in shimmering shafts, but none reached the wet, green twilight of the forest floor. Giant ferns seemed to float in the mist. Rose-red azaleas, twelve feet high and covered with clusters of spiked blossoms, crowded the trail.

"The West has its own cathedrals," her uncle Ralph Windemere, a medical missionary in Oregon Territory, had written, and Gloriana had imagined giant stone walls rising in the wilderness. Now she understood and rejoiced anew that she had answered his call for help at the Klamath Lake Mission; yet she could not suppress a small shiver of apprehension.

The way had not been easy. In 1851 the country had not forgotten the massacre of the Whitmans at their

5

Waiilatpu mission four years earlier. Moreover, the Mission Board had objected strenuously to sending an unmarried young lady—a "spinster," they had called her, although Gloriana was barely twenty-three—into the frontier. But she had persevered through appeal after appeal to the Foreign Missions Commissioners and through protest after protest from family and friends.

"If you hear the call of God, you must answer on the outside as well as the inside," she had told them all, and finally they had listened—perhaps as much because they could find no one else qualified to assist Dr. Windemere and willing to face the hostile native tribes as because they believed God had called Gloriana to be a missionary nurse.

Now, after months spent sailing around the Horn to San Francisco; days, plowing up the coast line on a small freighter to Crescent City in northern California, she was in the last stage of the journey, and her heart sang while her knees shook.

"These trees were here when Jesus was born in Bethlehem." She remembered with awe what her uncle had written about the great age of the redwoods. The fact made them seem closer to her and, somehow, less alien.

The grove they were passing through dwarfed the freight train. Mammoth trunks tapered to distant, sky-fringed tops. Where trees had been felled for the Crescent City-Jacksonville Trail, massive stumps, uprooted and dragged from the path, towered above the wagons. The tangle of moss-hung, black roots looked almost, but not quite, like the writhing tentacles of some prehistoric beast in the lingering mist.

"What a magnificent forest!" Gloriana voiced her impression, drawing a sardonic glance from the hulking driver.

"Good place for an ambush of hostiles," was his discouraging answer, and Gloriana thought she detected a malicious gleam in the corner of the driver's eye as she darted a startled look into the dark covert made by a particularly menacing fallen giant.

She had not liked Graham Norton from the first moment she had seen him, leaning against the rough redwood counter in the Siskiyou Freight Company office at Crescent City. That the antipathy had been both instantaneous and mutual was small consolation. He had at first refused to take her on his freight run to the gold fields at Jacksonville.

"No room," he had growled, looking Gloriana over from the top of her neatly bonneted head to her tightly buttoned boots—as though she, rather than the supplies sitting on the dock where the sailors had unloaded them would personally crowd him. He had relented only after much urging from the company agent and her own avowed purpose to hire other wagons and drivers.

But the battle lines had been drawn early on, and the hostilities had escalated throughout the afternoon as Gloriana supervised the loading of a small pump organ sent to the mission by her home church in Philadelphia and innumerable boxes and trunks—all and sundry of which the recalcitrant freighter had declared unsuitable for travel or unnecessary to existence on the frontier.

While seething with indignation, Gloriana had been unable to subdue a slight twinge of disappointment. Strange! She had never allowed herself much interest in men, thinking it would be futile folly. Handsome rather than beautiful, she was—in spite of her radiant name—the plain Jane of the family. Masses of dark hair, although silky and curling, were no match for her sister Juliana's corn-colored crown; and giant hazel eyes, although heavily fringed with black lashes, could not compete with her sister Marianna's china-blue orbs. If her complexion was creamy and her figure, tall and well-formed, they went unnoticed,

7

flanked by one sister's fairylike grace and the other's charming plumpness.

She had imagined, if only unconsciously, that in the West she might receive her share of admiration. In fact, her father, who cherished the delusion she was a general favorite, secretly admired by but forbidding to the young men of the church he pastored, had given his hopes that she would "find a man more to your taste" as a major reason for permitting the journey into Oregon Territory.

If Graham Norton were any indication, they had both been mistaken. He had taken one look at her fresh face, bare of cosmetics, and the trim, erect figure clad in the dove-colored garments Gloriana considered suitable for a traveling missionary and obviously pronounced her unfit. Well, she would show him—not that Graham Norton was at all the kind of man Gloriana Windemere would care to impress. Much larger than allowable for any degree of elegance, he reminded her of the surly grizzlies— called *ursus horribilis* or "devils in bears' clothing" by the settlers. Or a tawny cougar, as fierce and unscrupulous an animal as any in the Western woods, her Uncle Ralph said.

Nearly six feet, four inches in his stocking feet, Graham Norton conveyed a sense of the savage and untamed, less by his appearance and speech than by an aura of tense, leashed energy that surrounded him. His dress blended the fantastic and picturesque with the serviceable. A buckskin coat decorated with beading, dyed porcupine quills, and fringe opened over corduroy pants and a soft doeskin shirt. Instead of a tie, he wore a loosely knotted bandanna in a red paisley print. A flat-brimmed felt hat tilted back to reveal a mop of carelessly brushed, carrot-colored curls—much too long and garish for Gloriana's suddenly fastidious taste. Completing the barbaric picture, a black-handled gun with a menacingly long barrel protruded from a smooth leather holster beneath his coat, and a long-nosed rifle leaned against the wagon seat, suggestively close and ready.

"I'm sure the natives have learned their lesson," Gloriana commented with a careful air of unconcern. "The *Philadelphia Enquirer* carried a full account of the trial and hanging of the Indians who murdered the Whitmans." Her tone implied that he had probably never heard of the highly touted Eastern paper, or, if he had, was undoubtedly incapable of reading it.

His look was one of mingled impatience and contempt, and Gloriana noticed inconsequentially that his dark blue eyes had little golden flecks that made them seem to spark dangerously. His bronzed face was clean shaven and handsome, although the square cut of his jaw was in keeping with the obstinacy she had already experienced from the man.

"Yes, ma'am," was all he said, but he managed to infuse the two words with a host of negative comments on her ignorance of the West, her inability to understand the dangers of the situation, her unfitness for the life.

"Well, don't you agree that it's a mark of civilization's advance when a massacre is settled, not with more killings but by legal means?" Gloriana prodded him unwisely.

"Chief Telokite and his henchmen were hanged after the trial," Graham returned. "That's more killing. Besides, Cayuse law allows for the killing of bad medicine men. They considered Dr. Whitman bad. He let too many of their people die."

Gloriana lapsed into an offended silence, made all the more unbearable by the feeling that behind his sardonic mask this uncouth Westerner was laughing at her. The very idea of calling Dr. Whitman, one of the greatest medical missionaries of the age, a medicine man! And a bad one to boot! She refused to stoop to reply to such a ridiculous charge.

9

She wondered what Graham Norton would say if he knew she had come West to be her uncle's nurse. Somehow she doubted he would see her as an angel of mercy sacrificing a comfortable life in the East to minister to the Klamath Indians. He would probably imply that she was a goody-two-shoes, bent on bringing Saturday night baths and box socials to the West, or worse, an old maid come husband-hunting. Gloriana's cheeks burned at her own imaginings, and as though he could read her mind, Graham Norton chuckled, a deep, rich chuckle, totally out of keeping with the nature of the man.

The freight train in which they were traveling was a large one—twenty wagons in all, each drawn by teams of long-eared mules. Fifteen of the wagons were loaded with the supplies for Jacksonville, the new gold-boom town in the Rogue River Valley. The rest carried her trunks and the gifts from her father's church for the Klamath Lake Mission.

Glancing over her shoulder, Gloriana tried to catch sight of the wagon that carried the organ, but too many trees and giant ferns obscured the winding trail. She tried not to imagine that the frequent thumps and crashes she heard were branches, knocking against the precious instrument, or her trunks, bouncing from the wagon bed to be forgotten in the dense under-growth.

Gloriana was not the only passenger on the train. There were several prospectors, conspicuous for the pickaxes and shovels that figured prominently in their gear and the almost universal feature of bushy, uncut beards. Nor was she the only female. Three hard-featured women in bright-colored dresses, cut much too low for a wilderness trek, were traveling to the gold camps. No one had introduced them to Gloriana, but the men of the train, including Graham Norton, had clustered around them before the wagons had left Crescent City that morning, each driver apparently vying for the pleasure of their company. Somewhere behind Gloriana and Norton, the brittle laughter of one of the women mingled with the loud guffaws of a freighter, and Gloriana wondered why she had ended up traveling with the unpleasant train boss. Probably he had lost a bet, or perhaps it was his practice to take the most odious chores upon himself.

"What do you call these woods?" Gloriana turned to her companion with the determination to behave with civility and perhaps also with the half-formed hope that she could make him as uncomfortable as she.

Surprisingly, Norton responded with a running travelogue that required only her occasional word as the strong mule teams pulled their heavy loads along mile after mile of forest trail. True, he seemed to dwell unnecessarily long on accounts of massacres and scalpings. Once when they rumbled past a burned-out cabin, he gave her a detailed account of the warring customs of the Shasta tribe, including their throwing their victims into the burning throat of a volcano. And Gloriana listened in fascinated horror, although she remembered well her Uncle Ralph's assurance that the magnificent volcanos that towered over the region were extinct.

Gradually, as the morning wore on, the chilly mists dissolved, and a muggy warmth settled heavily around them. To Gloriana's shocked dismay, Norton removed his coat and, with a grin that acknowledged and relished her discomfort, drove on in his shirt sleeves. Back East a gentleman would not have appeared before a lady in his shirt sleeves. Many times Gloriana had seen her own father slip hastily into a coat when she or one of her sisters entered a room. But she was not back East now and Graham Norton was certainly not a gentleman. Gloriana sighed, sending a quick prayer toward heaven for the civilizing as well as the conversion of the West.

Heat in the rain forest was almost tangible. It penetrated the shade, rising in steamy waves from marshy puddles at the side of the trail and pricking the lungs on needle-spiced breaths. Perspiration beaded the skin and stayed there, wet and sticky, refusing to evaporate in the humid air.

Although she debated how ladylike it would be to ride uncovered, Gloriana at last removed her poke bonnet and set it neatly in her lap. She had never been a prude, but she could not bring herself to unfasten her cuffs and collar; the very freedom of her surroundings seemed to have afflicted her with inhibitions she had never dreamed of before. Or perhaps it was her companion. Surprised to see an appreciative look at the glossy braids wound in a crown around her head, she hid the mounting color in her cheeks by dabbing at the perspiration on her forehead with a lace-edged handkerchief.

It was a relief to stop for the noon break. The redwoods were gradually giving way to firs and pines as the wagons climbed steadily away from the coast, and with the smaller trees more of the sun's hot rays found their way to the forest floor. Pebbles, instead of sand, lined the white-water creek where the mules splashed and drank, thankful, it seemed, to be out of harness and less eager for their feedbags than for the soothing touch of the water.

The creek was cold in spite of the day's heat, and Gloriana wondered how quickly it must have come from some snow-capped peak not to share the torpor and sluggishness that humans and animals alike felt. She ate as much as she could swallow of what the camp cook offered her. A short, stocky teamster, with midcalf boots and a floppy hat that nearly covered his eyebrows—he had piled her plate with enough stew and biscuits to feed a family. She had looked from his cheerful face to his grimy hands and accepted the whole along with his admonition to "eat up." But her quick blessing included a reminder of the Lord's promise: "If ye eat any deadly thing, it shall not hurt you."

Wandering away from the other travelers, Gloriana found a quiet place, just out of sight of the camp. She leaned back against a tree trunk at the edge of the stream, luxuriating in the feel of the deliciously cool air on her face and neck. She had closed her eyes and was drinking in the musical sounds of the water, thrumming along its pebble bed, when a rough hand closed over her shoulder and jerked her to her feet. Then an arm, corded with muscles, fastened around her waist, and she looked up into the gleaming blue eyes of wagon boss Graham Norton.

He was stripped to the waist and wet, as though he had been washing in the stream. For a moment Gloriana felt a shiver, either of fear or of excitement, travel down her spine before a surge of fury reminded her of her dignity and her rights.

"How—" she started, but had barely gotten the first word out when he crushed her against him and kissed her—a quick, hard pressure of his lips.

"How dare you!" she choked it out this time.

"Shut up and look over my shoulder." His muttered response startled her nearly as much as his actions.

Standing just within the shadow of the forest, barely ten yards away on the other side of the shallow stream, was a band of Indian braves. Whether there were a dozen or fifty Gloriana was too frightened to tell. But she could clearly see the bands of war paint slanting down their cheeks. The feather-decked spears in their hands looked no less menacing because they pointed skyward instead of in her direction.

"Turn around slowly and walk back toward camp. Don't look back. I'll be right behind you." Norton released her with a little shove that sent her stumbling backward. She imagined she heard muffled laughter

13

from the braves as she retreated in a less-than-dignified manner. She knew that she felt their eyes and Graham Norton's burrowing into her back, noting the red flush creeping up the back of her neck, and enjoying her discomfiture.

The teamsters and other passengers looked at them curiously as Gloriana and Graham Norton appeared. Gloriana thought she caught the exchange of a knowing look between two of the women, but the incident was quickly forgotten as Norton explained the presence of the Indians—''renegades,'' he said, which seemed to carry some special significance for the men. The order to harness the mules was scarcely necessary; the drivers had already begun pulling the reluctant animals toward the wagons.

The party was large and well-armed. Most had fought in more than one Indian war, but the experiences had taught them to be cautious rather than overconfident. They broke camp quickly, leaving the remains of a generous meal to tempt the war party. No one knew how many more braves might be hiding along the trail, waiting for them or following invisibly through the forest. The men drove with their reins in their left hands and their rifles cradled across their knees, but the intelligent mules had caught a sense of urgency tinged with fear from their drivers and found their own way along the trail, staying as close to the wagon before them as the great, lumbering loads of freight would allow.

Graham Norton's wagon had taken the lead. No one had thought to direct Gloriana to another seat, so she had scrambled up beside him and tried to supplement the keen looks he shot into the forest with an intense scrutiny of her own. She thought about offering to drive the mules, for she had often driven a team of horses, once taking an ambulance wagon from the scene of a factory fire to the hospital. But she doubted her ability to drive four-in-hand, and the mules seemed less obliging than the more-familiar horses.

The trail broke unexpectedly into a mountain meadow, and the momentary relief at escaping the confines of the forest with its myriad hiding places gave way to panic at being exposed to invisible eyes, watching from a thousand trees at the forest edge or on the hillsides overlooking the clearing. Once Gloriana thought she saw a dark head dart back around a tree trunk; she grasped Norton's arm and nodded in the direction of a massive escarpment, not knowing whether she should continue the fiction of being oblivious to the savages' presence. He said nothing but quickened the pace of the team.

Late in the afternoon a teamster misjudged a sharp turn and a load of mission supplies, although fortunately not the organ, tumbled down the hillside. Gloriana heard the sharp scream of the woman passenger and was out of the wagon before Norton could stop his mules and set the hand brake.

The woman had been thrown clear, but she was stunned, and her arm had bent under her as she fell. The driver was pinned under the wagon and from the angle of his pelvis, wedged under the heavy wheel rim, Gloriana thought broken bones would be the least of his trouble.

"You there, help me move this woman." Gloriana took charge as she would have at home in the Philadelphia hospital, calling on the amiable cook who rushed forward to help. "Don't right that wagon until you have pulled the driver out," she cautioned the teamsters. "We'll have to make camp now," she informed Graham Norton as he hurried up with his rifle still in the crook of his arm.

He looked at her intensely a moment, then nodded. "There's a place not far ahead. We'll get this wagon right side up and put them in it. We'll come back for your boxes."

"I'll have to find some of the medical supplies," she told him.

He sent a man with her to find a box marked with red crosses, containing, she hoped, the bandages, splints, and antiseptics she would need.

The box had rolled nearly to the foot of the brush-covered hill. As Gloriana bent over it, she spotted the soft gray-brown toe of a moccasin protruding slightly from a covert of grasses and manzanita. She glanced quickly at her companion to see if he had noticed, but the teamster was busy hoisting the heavy box. Breathing a quick prayer for help, Gloriana grabbed hold of another, smaller package that looked like the medical bag her father had sent his brother and scrambled up the hill without a backward glance.

CHAPTER 2

PRACTICING MEDICINE under the open sky by star and firelight would have seemed impossible to Gloriana if she had had time to think about it. Two dozen men lounged nearby as she prepared her instruments. Ordinarily their obvious expressions of distrust would have angered her, but the situation was too bizarre for ordinary reactions.

The woman's injury would be easiest to deal with. The fall had broken her arm, but the fracture was clean, with no bone perforating the skin. The teamster's injuries, as she had feared, were more serious. A rib had torn its way through the skin, the pelvic bone was bruised but thankfully not shattered, and there were signs of some internal bleeding.

Lord, I'm not a doctor; I'm just a nurse, Gloriana sent her protests heavenward, knowing full well that however inadequate she might be, she was all the help these people had.

She worked slowly, feeling her way. One of the men who had once served as a hospital orderly came forward to help, and she directed him to hold the injured driver as she manipulated and taped the broken rib, then sewed up the gash in his side and applied a pressure bandage to stop the bleeding.

The woman provided more resistance since she was conscious and feeling the pain. "Don't hurt me," she whimpered. Then more belligerently, she demanded Gloriana leave the break for the doctor in Jacksonville to set. "I can't chance it not being done correct-like," she explained. Gloriana realized she did not mean to offend but was attempting to reason with her. "I ain't got no one else to take care of me and I havta play the piany at the Golden Horse Saloon."

She was just past youth. A fine etching of crow's feet radiated from eyes that burned in pale skin. The thin arms and hollow chest suggested a consumptive tendency and an intolerance to the alcohol such women usually depended upon. Gloriana had seen it often in the street women of Philadelphia, and she supposed their end was likely to be the same whether they were in the city or on the frontier.

"Perhaps you could sing for a while," she began talking soothingly while her fingers probed the swollen arm.

The woman—Rita was her name, she said, "just plain Rita with no fancy handle after it"—seemed to consider the suggestion but rejected it for one of her own. "I maybe could deal blackjack. I'm good at that and the gents always like to see a purty gal at the table."

The former orderly, who had worked quietly during most of the evening, spoke up in a voice that was surprisingly gentle. He assured Rita that he would be happy to play at her table, and, if her boss at the Golden Horse didn't like it, he would buy her her own saloon with the gold he planned to find. Gloriana glanced at her helper with a new respect and decided a woman like Rita might be better off on the frontier after all.

The bone was easy enough to set. Rita's frail arm provided little resistance as they pulled the edges into place. But the operation took all the strength Gloriana had left, and she was trembling with fatigue when she bound some of the mission's splints tightly around the broken arm and asked the orderly/miner to give Rita some of the herb tea Gloriana used to fight fever.

By midnight most of the company had fallen asleep, but the campfire burned brightly, casting eerie flame-shaped shadows over the wagons and tents. Gloriana sank down on a wooden box that someone had placed close to the fire. She noticed for the first time that the wagons had been turned in a circle, warding off but not quite excluding the darkness outside. They were in a cleared area, not a meadow, for manzanita and scrub juniper bunched thickly around the wagons. A few ragged widow-makers, as they called burned timber in the logging camps, made darker gashes against the gray night sky.

Night sounds were magnified in the darkness. Somewhere close by, another creek, or perhaps the same one they had followed for much of the afternoon, rilled its way through the wilderness. Crickets seemed to have moved into the camp, and their creaky fiddling sounded from the rocks that bounded the fire. And around the camp the bushes and dead leaves rustled with nameless scurryings.

"Would you like some coffee?" Graham Norton asked the question a second time before Gloriana could stir herself to answer. She accepted the hot tin cup he offered, conscious of his curious gaze on her face, and wondered rather remotely if her hair had come undone or her rolled-up sleeves showed too much of her round, capable arms.

"I want to apologize," he started after a moment. "I did not know you were a doctor."

Gloriana looked at him, bewildered for a moment, then remembered his remarks earlier in the day about bad medicine men. "I'm not," she told him with a tired smile and sipped the scalding coffee. The tin cup burned her fingers, and she held it carefully around the rim.

"You can't tell me you learned how to do what you did this evening in your fancy ladies' seminary."

"I'm a nurse," she told him finally, recalling her determination earlier in the day not to expose herself to this man's ridicule. Now it didn't seem to matter. "I've never had to do so much alone before, but I think they'll be all right." After a moment she added with a little laugh, "And I've never been to a fancy ladies' seminary."

He grinned rather sheepishly, and the expression lightened his face, dropping years from the hard, if handsome, features. Since the day before Gloriana had watched mask after mask cover that face—unreachable obstinacy when he was refusing her request for transportation, sardonic humor as he needled her on the ride through the redwoods, grim determination when they fled from the renegade Indians. Now she imagined she was seeing the real Graham Norton behind the facades of the invincible Westerner, and she could not help admitting his was a good face—strong but not quite invulnerable; serious, without being humorless.

"We lost most of your supplies," he told her, seemingly not a little embarrassed by the fact. "We found the places where they had been dragged into the forest, but the boxes had been broken open and were empty. It would have taken fifty braves at least to carry that much stuff away."

Gloriana told him then about the moccasined foot she had spotted in the brush.

"They must have been shadowing the trail, waiting for a chance. Lucky for us it came before they attacked. Too bad about those supplies, though." He came back to the sore spot with a persistence that told

20

Gloriana more than any words could how much responsibility and accomplishment meant to this man. He had not wanted to take her load on the freight train he was bossing, but having accepted the extra duty, he hated to admit failure. Besides, he was probably in the best position right then to judge the true worth of Eastern-made goods in the wilderness, and he realized better than Gloriana how difficult they would be to replace.

"Most of those things were intended for the Indians anyway," she told him with a little shrug. "They just got there in a different way than we planned."

Norton showed her the lean-to that had been built for her comfort just outside the circle of firelight. She hoped she would have a chance to use it, but the teamster was in danger and would require nursing through the night. This was the work Gloriana did best, and she settled to it, thankful to be back on familiar ground after the unaccustomed demands on her skills earlier in the evening.

Gloriana liked best to keep watch in the night. Whether there were stars overhead or a soft lamp at her elbow, she felt most in charge in the dim light. Usually she would pray softly through the hours between midnight and dawn, stopping only to change the cold compresses with which she sought to temper a fever or to administer a dose of medicine at the prescribed hour. Most often she had watched with children—and looking thoughtfully at the injured man's face for the first time, she was struck by how near a child he was.

The valiant attempt at a manly beard on his chin showed more fuzz than bush. The dark lashes curling against his cheeks looked absurdly boyish, and several times during the long hours of watching and praying, Gloriana heard a whispered appeal for "Ma."

The crisis passed just before dawn. Noting the even

rhythm of her patient's breathing and the reassuring dampness of his skin, Gloriana thanked God. Her other patient, though not in danger, seemed to be suffering more, but a careful sponging with water from the cold stream and more of the special herb tea eased her discomfort.

Her patient's needs cared for, Gloriana allowed herself the luxury of a stretch and went looking for the traveling bag she had packed for the trip. She found it just inside the lean-to of evergreen boughs on her unused bedroll. Taking a fresh blouse and her toilet things, she headed for the stream.

With the experience of the previous noon still fresh in her mind, she chose a little backwater, well screened from the opposite bank as well as from the camp, and removed only part of her clothing. She was dismayed at the grime that had accumulated in just one day on the dusty woodland trail and hoped her supply of soap had not been among the items pilfered the day before. The dirt responded to her ministrations, but her hair proved recalcitrant. The humid mountain air had kinked the masses into showers of curls that refused the discipline of braids. Finally she settled for tying it back from her face with a ribbon, and with a clean blouse and sponged skirt, she felt refreshed.

She had hardly finished when she was startled by the massive frame of Graham Norton, stepping through the bushes. Her first thought—that he had been spying on her—was not altogether dismissed by the look of surprise on his face.

The circumstances reminded her uncomfortably of the incident of the day before, and after answering his questions about the injured members of his company, she determined to make her dissatisfaction with his methods, if not, she hoped, his motives, clear.

"I want to thank you for . . . coming to my rescue yesterday," Gloriana began with dignity but could not

22

bring herself to look directly into those piercing, gold-flecked eyes. I had no chance to mention it before." She thought of the night before, when she *could* have mentioned it and started again. "That is, it didn't occur to me before. I mean, I know I should not have wandered away from the group like that, and I appreciate your sparing me from any unpleasant consequences of my actions. However, I must say that does not excuse such behavior. I want you to know that I do not condone liberties . . . ."

A grin had been growing on Norton's face through-out the latter part of this speech—a grin so mocking and mischievous that it would have fully unnerved Gloriana if she had happened to glance up and see it. Now Norton cut her short with an explosive laugh.

"You don't have to thank me any more, lady," he managed between chuckles. "It wasn't half bad. You can take liberties with my person any time you feel like it. Besides, I figured if those braves thought you already belonged to someone, they wouldn't be so ready to start a fight over you. But as it turned out, it wasn't you, after all, but our supplies they wanted."

Speechless with rage, Gloriana glared up into Graham Norton's mocking face, and before she knew what she was doing, her hand had come up in a resounding slap across his cheek. The blow sobered him instantly, and she shrank from the menace in his eyes.

"You had no call to do that, Glory," he told her quietly.

"Don't you dare call me Glory!" she burst out, and then, on the verge of tears, turned and ran toward the camp.

The scene that greeted her was so unexpected it wiped the humiliation of her encounter with Graham Norton from her mind. The teamsters were breaking camp. Already the main tent had been felled and the mules were being hitched to the wagon. The cook spotted Gloriana and motioned her cheerfully toward a plate of food he had saved for her by the fire. But he too was moving swiftly, packing utensils and carving fist-sized sandwiches to be eaten on the trail.

"They can't just go," she appealed in bewilderment to Graham Norton, who had followed her from the creek.

"Don't worry, Miss Windemere. We won't leave you behind," he assured her coldly, his stern Western mask now firmly in place.

"I'm not worried about myself," she turned on him fiercely. "We have sick people here. They cannot be moved. I won't allow it."

"You have nothing to say about it. We can't stay here, and neither can they."

"You don't understand," she tried again, imagining that his ignorance kept him from grasping the situation. "That young man may die if we move him."

"No, ma'am, you're the one who doesn't understand," he said, brushing her hand away from his arm where she had laid it in her earnestness. "Those Indians trailing us are renegades and killers. They are at war with all white men, and their war code does not permit any prisoners but women.

"If we go, one man may die. If we stay, we may all die, and you and the other women can look forward to a life spent in a wickiup if you catch some brave's eye, or, if you don't, a few days of hell on earth, then a tomahawk in the back of your skull . . . . We're pulling out."

CHAPTER 3

THE FREIGHT TRAIN MOVED FORWARD that second day with a watchful grimness that underscored the seriousness of their plight. Already the hostile braves could have hidden their stolen goods, to return on swift, unburdened feet. They would have no trouble finding the trail, of course. The freight company had slashed a way through the forest that none could miss, and in spite of wagon boss Norton's caution to move quietly with a minimum of talk, twenty heavily loaded wagons drawn by forty stomping, braying mules could undoubtedly be heard for miles.

Gloriana rode with her patients in the nearly empty bed of the same wagon that had overturned the day before. There was little she could do to cushion the bumps and jostling. The freight wagon had no springs and, minus its heavy load of the ill-fated mission supplies, the wagon bed bounced with each rut, rock, and ridge in the trail.

The injured but now-conscious teamster rode better than Gloriana would have believed possible. During the day she learned that he was eighteen years old, that his name was George Mulligan, and that he considered it unmanly to lie in a wagon bed while the company ran for its life through the woods. When Gloriana refused to allow him to return to the driver's seat, he capitulated at the price of being allowed to have his rifle ready beside him. He would not have been able to sit up if she had agreed, but somehow his insistence and her refusal made his incapacity more acceptable.

Rita had a fever, but the color of the bruised skin of her arm around the splinted and bandaged break looked all right. Still, Gloriana could not be sure, and she wished hopelessly for a doctor to consult and prayed hopefully for the end of the trek to come soon.

She had no way of knowing how far away from a settlement of any kind they were—which was, perhaps, fortunate, for if she could have foreseen the hard days of travel, the mountain range to be climbed, and the rivers to be forded, her courage might have failed long before it did.

But if her courage and strength failed, her faith grew. Days passed, the Indians did not attack, and she thanked the Lord. After a few hard nights of watching beside their beds, she saw her patients' bouts with fever break, and their injuries show signs of proper healing. "There is much to be thankful for," Gloriana reminded herself when her backside ached from long hours of riding on rough board seats; her skin burned and peeled, leaving her with a shockingly unfeminine tan; and her feet blistered from walking beside the wagon as the mules pulled and strained their way up steep hillsides.

To occupy her hands and her mind, Gloriana dug out the journal she had begun on shipboard and started to recount the days since they had left Crescent City.

It is now eight days since we started our journey. So far we have been chased by Indians, suffered a wagon accident, and endured a variety of hardships, nonetheless trying because they were foreseen. Everything is somehow bearable except for the dirt. It rises in clouds from the trail, sifting through tightly laced boots to be ground into the heels and toes of stockings and burrowing through the clothes to smear the skin with a scratchy layer. I would give anything for a hot, soapy bath and the chance to wash my hair properly.

The people of the freight train are a motley assortment of adventurers, pioneers, and lost souls who have wandered to the edges of civilization searching for identity and acceptance.

The more I see of them, the more I become convinced of the need for missions in Oregon Territory. On Sunday I was permitted to read a verse of Scripture and pray over the company before the day's journey, but even George Mulligan and the cook laughed when I reminded them that the Lord would have us rest on His day. I shudder to think what a wasteland these pioneers will make of their glorious land if women do not come to make the family the center of Western life and ministers do not come to remind them that this land, like all others, is God's.

On the fourteenth day of their journey, the trail broke from the forest, and the train rolled into a lush, green valley dotted with log cabins and presided over by an impressive timbered blockhouse and fort.

The coming of a freight train was apparently a great event in this frontier community. Women in gingham gowns hurried from the cabins, wiping their hands on their checkered aprons. Men in straw hats and overalls looked up from their work in barns or fields. Barefoot children ran after the wagons, ignoring the teamsters' gruff reminders to stay away from the mules' hooves.

Called Applegate Landing for its founders, the settlement boasted, in addition to the fort, a general store, a combination flour and sawmill, and a brand-new, whitewashed church with a steeple and a small bell. Most of the structures were made of logs, stacked and chinked and capped by a heavy roof of shake shingles, but a few of the leading citizens had built salt-box houses of planed boards from the mill and whitewashed them in imitation of the new church. Minute yards, filled with every variety of eastern flower that could be coaxed to grow in the acidic valley soil, held out the wilderness with prim picket fences.

To her surprise Gloriana found herself something of a celebrity to the inhabitants.

"We know your uncle well," a jovial older man told her as he commandeered her and a trunk that she pointed out as absolutely essential to her comfort, and shepherded both toward a large white house on the edge of the settlement. His status in the community was suggested by the string tie and black suit he wore in spite of the informality of his surroundings, and she soon learned that he was Jesse Applegate, frontiersman, man of letters, and pioneer, who had figured largely in Uncle Ralph's letters as the Sage of the Yoncalla, the location of his land claim.

His wife, Cynthia Ann, made Gloriana welcome in a two-story home that denied its presence in the wilderness. Frilled curtains framed glass windows, and figured carpets softened the hardwood floors.

"I never really wanted to leave Missouri," she told Gloriana, "so Jesse promised me that here in the house it would seem as though I were back home." And indeed, if it had not been for the tangled forest and the rather ominous blockhouse of the fort, visible from the windows, the Applegate house would have seemed like any of the farm houses Gloriana had visited in the Pennsylvania countryside.

Oddly enough, she felt a little let down. Her uncle had built a legend of the Applegates as one of the first families of the Oregon Territory, and her own active

28

imagination had added a semi-barbaric picture of Daniel-Boone-type figures and primitive surroundings liberally decorated with bear skins, buffalo robes, and Indian rugs.

But it was heaven to enjoy the luxury of a tub bath and clean clothes from the skin out. Unexpectedly, Gloriana's hostess urged her to hurry rather than to relax and pamper herself. It seemed that a company of soldiers had arrived in the settlement, dispatched by Army Headquarters at Fort Winnemucca to protect the settlers from the same renegades who had stolen Gloriana's supplies. So many visitors at one time had inspired the hospitable Applegates to sponsor a banquet on the town square, to be followed by a country dance. Gloriana was urged to put on her prettiest dress and offered rice powder to disguise the rosy tan which her pioneer-style poke bonnet had not kept from her face and neck.

She agreed to the former and politely rejected the latter, rather liking the look of unaccustomed color in her usually pale face. She was rather startled to notice that the prospect of an evening of dancing in this remote frontier community, under the shadow of danger and the threat of Indian raids, had nonetheless left her excited and eager to look her best. She wondered absently who would ask her to dance. Would Graham Norton be there? If so, would he expect her to dance with him? If he did, what would she say? Or not say? What would he say or not say? They had barely spoken for days after she had slapped him (she winced at that memory); yet he had been friendly enough before they reached Applegate Landing. Did that mean he had forgiven and forgotten? Hadn't he begun to show an interest in her that went beyond her status as a passenger on his wagon train?

Thus the time before the festivities were to begin passed quickly and pleasantly, the anxieties of preparation balanced by the anticipation of minor triumphs.

When she left the Applegates' house at dusk, walking confidently between the effusively friendly couple, Gloriana knew she looked her best—and in fact, for the first time in her life came close to living up to her rather intimidating name.

Her dress was a simple muslin, sprigged in cherry on a lighter background with its chief ornament a deep, gathered flounce at the hem that would look nice, Gloriana knew, as she twirled in dancing. But if the dress was simpler than Mrs. Applegate, hungering for Eastern fashion, had hoped for, the cut was elegant and set off Gloriana's tall figure. The sleeves were puffed; the neckline, square and modest, but exposing an expanse of creamy skin. Gloriana added a pink coral necklace of carved roses, given her long ago by her grandmother, and tucked matching rosette stickpins in the curls which she had piled on top of her head.

"Gloriana Windemere is a remarkably pretty girl," she heard Jesse Applegate tell his wife, and for possibly the first time in her life, Gloriana felt "remarkably" pretty. She had, of course, been to many parties in Philadelphia, but always she had been cast in the shadow by her entrancing sisters. Still, this evening she felt she could have competed with Juliana and Marianna at their best. Moreover, she had a wonderful consciousness of being like these Westerners—strong, intelligent, resourceful, able to contribute something to the new world and to build and defend a home in the wilderness.

Tables had been laid beneath a stand of pines. The fallen needles made a pleasantly cushioned carpet, and nearby pitchy trunks filled the air with a spicy scent. Bonfires to be lit later had been laid in cleared circles, and someone had thoughtfully placed round sections of sawed tree trunks for seating around the grassy area that would serve as a dance floor.

Gloriana saw Graham Norton lounging beside a

30

barbecue pit where great strips of beef and pork and whole chickens turning on spits were roasting. His immediate, if offhand, wave said that he had seen her first, and Gloriana imagined there was an interest in the gaze he fixed on her that had not been there before.

The woodland banquet hall and ballroom would have been attractive at any time of the day, but at dusk an enchantment settled over the place. Far down the river valley to the west, a watercolor sunset brightened the soft twilight sky with glorious smears of orange, rose, and red. In the soft shadows of the trees, lamps beckoned and voices seemed unnaturally magnified, causing speakers to lower their voices to a soft murmur.

"How perfectly magnificent!" Gloriana breathed softly, then flushed in embarrassment as hearty male laughter greeted her words. She realized belatedly that Mrs. Applegate was trying to present a young uniformed officer to her distracted guest.

"I have been given cordial welcomes before, but I don't believe anyone has ever called me 'magnificent,'" he laughed down into Gloriana's upturned face. "'Dashing' perhaps or even 'charming' but never 'magnificent.'"

Gloriana joined the laughter at her expense, all the while wondering why Lieutenant John Tilton seemed so instantly familiar, as though they had met a day or a week before. He was as handsome as only a uniform seems to make some men. Straight black hair covered his forehead and just touched the top of his collar. His face was a ruddy tan that made his flashing smile literally dazzling. And there was something in his eyes—a spark, a glint, a gleam of deviltry—that stirred a sense of adventure and danger in Gloriana.

"Haven't we met somewhere before?" she finally asked him.

"Here now, that's supposed to be my line," he told

her and, somehow securing hold of her arm, Lieutenant Tilton drew Gloriana away from their beaming hostess. "You're supposed to say, 'Pleased to meet you,' and I say, 'You have been in my dreams from the first moment we met at the garden party or the symphony or the box social.'"

Gloriana laughed again and was not totally displeased to notice that Graham Norton was watching them intently from across the grassy dance floor.

"More probably if we did meet at all, it was during one of the West Point balls," she told the lieutenant, looking over her shoulder in what she hoped was a fair imitation of her sister Juliana's best flirtatious manner. "My youngest brother entered the Point three years ago, and he often invited us for the balls."

"How extraordinary to meet a lady of social distinction in this God-forsaken place! Tell me why you are here, and promise me you will not leave, no matter how dreary the days and the company."

"But God has not forsaken this place," Gloriana countered quickly, not noticing the officer's skirting the question of whether or not they might have met at West Point. "That is why I am here. I'm to join my Uncle Ralph Windemere in his mission at Klamath Lake."

Lieutenant Tilton, it turned out, knew her uncle and was full of news about the general locale of the mission. If his account lacked details about the mission work or praise for Dr. Windemere's accomplishments, Gloriana could excuse him, for what young man was as enthusiastic about church work and good deeds as about military life, battles, and guns?

The evening wore on and Gloriana met the residents of the settlement; ate roast beef, Oregon cheddar cheese, fresh bread, and huckleberry pie; listened to reminiscences about homes left long ago in Pennsylvania, Ohio, or Missouri; and shared what news she could remember—all, it seemed, with Lieutenant

32

Tilton at her elbow, acting the part of old and privileged friend, even though he did not claim it.

When the music of fiddles and guitars began, he demanded the first and then the second dance and would have insisted upon a third, but Gloriana turned him aside with a laughing reminder about the impropriety, well understood in the East, of a young lady's dancing more than twice with the same gentleman.

Although the lieutenant protested that the West was less restrictive—the one characteristic of the region that he seemed to approve—he surrendered her to her host who danced with her once himself, then introduced a string of eager partners, mostly fresh-faced young farmers.

It was late and the bonfires were burning low before Graham Norton approached her. He had been on the edge of the festivities all evening. When she had not seen him, Gloriana had felt him there, watching her with his inscrutable eyes. He didn't wait to ask but grasped her around the waist and swung her out onto the grass. Numerous couples continued to dance, although a late-rising moon had already begun its descent, and Gloriana's feet ached with the unaccustomed activity.

"You seem to be having a good time for yourself," was his opening conversational gambit, so unlike the teasing flattery she had been listening to all evening that Gloriana was too taken aback to reply.

"Like the pretty-faced lieutenant a lot, don't you?" he continued in the same vein.

"I don't see that it is any of your affair," Gloriana told him haughtily and drew back slightly from his clasp, which threatened to become more of an embrace than the light touch demanded by decorum. She tilted her head back to look up into the marble-smooth face and was surprised to see an open earnestness there instead of the mocking indifference she had expected.

Suddenly he swung her behind the shelter of a broad tree trunk. She thought for a moment he was going to kiss her. Their faces were close, almost touching; her heart pounded with abandon and she imagined she could hear his beating rapidly, too.

Instead, he moved back a foot, letting his arm drop from her waist but keeping her hand tightly in his, as though he were afraid she would try to run away.

"Glory, I shouldn't say anything. You're a female and likely to blab what you know. But I can't see you make a fool of yourself. Stay away from John Tilton! He's not what he seems."

Whatever reaction he expected, it was certainly not the wild fury that Gloriana unleashed upon him. That he should presume to dictate to her was past tolerating. That he should criticize her behavior, suggest that she was making a fool of herself, was beyond belief.

She told him in terms no less certain because they were ladylike that he had no right to speak to her about such things, that he should mind his own business, that a gentleman always faces one he accuses, and, for good measure, that she hoped she would never see him again.

"And don't call me Glory!"

CHAPTER 4

WATERY SUNLIGHT, DAMPENED BY EARLY VALLEY MISTS, flowed through the thick windowpanes of the Applegate guest room. Feeling its soft touch on her face and the crisp roughness of muslin sheets, Gloriana awoke, half expecting to hear her sisters, chattering in the room across the hall. Somewhere outside, a rooster greeted the morning. Bird choruses twittered and chirruped in the nearby treetops. From somewhere in the distance came the sharp rhythmic cracking of an ax splitting wood. It was almost like a summer morning in Philadelphia—but not quite.

Gloriana opened her eyes wide, remembering where she was and savoring the differences as the physical evidence of her adventure. She was lying in a pink-and-gold nest, like her bedroom back home. A flowered carpet on the floor waited to receive her bare feet. A gilt mirror hung over the white porcelain washbasin, and sprigs of pink flowers adorned the white water pitcher—cracked ever so slightly around the rim. But no Philadelphia bedroom had furniture of the rosy, streaked wood Gloriana was coming to

35

recognize as the rich, heavy heart of the redwood; nor had she ever awakened back home with the strong infuriating face of Graham Norton vividly in her mind.

"How dare he?" she fumed, once again, not quite willing to examine whether she was angry because the freighter had presumed to lecture her or because she had imagined he was thinking about romance when he only wanted to deliver his unwelcome advice.

The incidents of the night before seemed intensified rather than subdued by the daylight. Gloriana's face grew hot as she tried to remember her actions, wondering if she had perhaps forgotten herself in the excitement of these Westerners' admiration and behaved with too much abandon. What had she said? What had she done? Had she laughed too much? Danced too much? Her eyes closed, and she tried to call up a picture of herself, dancing with her usual gracious reserve. Instead, her relentless morning-after conscience replied with the image of a romping hoyden. "Gloriana Windemere, you had better get hold of yourself," she scolded, bouncing out of bed to face her image in the gilt-framed mirror.

The reflection that looked back hardly seemed that of a sedate missionary nurse. Her hair, which persisted in curling in the damp Oregon air, had pulled itself out of her bedtime braids to riot in dark profusion around her face. Her suntanned cheeks were rosy and her lips a bright red. Even the usually modest flannel nightdress had come open at the top in a daring décolletage.

Gloriana sighed, hoping her behavior had not damaged her Christian witness. "We have to be sure you can present the proper picture of Christ and the church," the Missionary Board had said when they had first rejected her application. At the time she had considered their caution an expression of narrow minds and a narrow religion. Now she wondered if perhaps they had had some experience with the effect of the frontier on young, unmarried women—"spinsters"—she recalled with a little grimace.

In any case, she was one spinster who was going to take herself in hand before it was too late. And not without a sense of the humor of the situation, Gloriana set about transforming the belle of last night's ball into once again the proper young missionary. She tamed her wayward curls into a sedate crown of braids, donned one of the dove-colored dresses that made her look like her Pilgrim forebears, and even applied some of Mrs. Applegate's rice powder to tone down the color in her complexion.

"That should be enough to discourage anyone," she told the thoroughly proper and, she had to admit, thoroughly dull-looking reflection in the mirror when the transformation was complete. She had no doubt that, put in her place, her sisters Juliana and Marianna would have made the most of their position as single women on a frontier teeming with men, but she was equally certain that becoming a Western belle was not what the Mission Board would want—although perhaps they expected it. For the sake of the other young women who might apply for mission posts, she would have to be doubly careful to "abstain from all appearance of evil."

"This is one Cinderella who won't become a princess," Gloriana told herself with a little laugh, but she could not resist wondering: if she had been Cinderella last night, who had been the prince— Graham Norton or John Tilton? She made a face at her prim reflection before turning away from the mirror.

She noticed again the beauty of the little room. It seemed to be bathed in a special light, which Gloriana soon discovered was from the thick glass in the latticework windows. The heavy panes, instead of transmitting the light, refracted it slightly to send glimmering rainbows dancing across the walls and floors. The effect was lovely but made her realize how difficult it must be to get something as ordinary as window glass in a frontier settlement like Applegate Landing.

In one corner, wreathed with rainbows, someone had made an old-fashioned prayer altar. A little picture of Christ hung on the wall, and beside that, a beautiful cross carved from a gold-colored wood Gloriana had never seen before. A rocking chair and footstool of the same glowing wood sat beside a night stand that held a well-worn Bible.

Sitting in the chair, she rocked for a few minutes and let the peace of the little haven flow through her. How often in the last few weeks and months had she forgotten the reason for her coming to the Oregon Territory? First, there had been the battles with the Mission Board and objections of her own family to overcome, then the packing and traveling and meeting new people. (She would not let herself single out anyone specifically.) But she was not here by accident. In fact, she could remember the first moment she had felt called.

The whole family had been sitting in the parlor one Sunday. They had been pursuing the quiet occupations that Philadelphia and her father's church considered proper for a sabbath. Gloriana's fingers had been quietly occupied in embroidering, but her mind was far from being quiet or sedate. She was thinking about the people and places in the letter from which her father had been reading. It had been from Uncle Ralph, and he had, as always, been effusive in his praise of the people and the land of his beloved Oregon Territory.

"I wish I could transplant every Eastern sapling into this rich land," he had said, "I guarantee that they would grow taller and stronger."

They had laughed at her uncle's favorite image of young people like trees taking root in the West.

"I hear some young ladies are having trouble finding suitable husbands in Philadelphia. If so, it's because all the finest young men have come West."

The girls, including Gloriana, had all blushed at that, and Marianna had looked indignant. She considered her favorite suitor, Morris von Pelter, a very fine man indeed, but it was difficult to imagine him as anything except a primly efficient bank teller in a primly efficient bank.

"You have heard the phrase 'noble redman,'" Uncle Ralph had continued. "Nothing better describes the Klamaths, Modocs, and Shastas—the people whose ancestors have lived in these forests for thousands of years. Although not originally Christians, the hunger for God is so great among them that they begged for the missionaries to come." And then he had described the poverty and illnesses—the epidemics of the white man's diseases, which to the unprepared immune systems of the Indians brought almost certain death.

She had not heard a loud or even a still, small voice call her, but when Uncle Ralph had mentioned his need of a nurse, she had known as surely as anything that here was something she could do, was meant to do, perhaps had even been born to do.

"I will go," she had said very quietly. Her father had looked stunned, her mother had begun to argue, and Juliana had said slyly, "She wants one of Uncle's fine young men; none of those here are good enough for her." But no arguments, mockery, or hardships had stopped her.

"And here I am," Gloriana reminded herself, looking out the window at the thick forests and the rounded cone of a volcano that towered over the valley. Yet honesty demanded that she examine her sister's charge. Was she really here first and foremost to find a husband? "Am I more interested in the Western men than I am in the native people?" she

39

asked half-aloud, thinking back over the days on the trail with Graham Norton, reminding herself uncomfortably of her reactions to his physical presence and touch. She remembered her pleasure the night before, the excitement of being, for the first time in her life, the belle of the party. Then she shifted her focus to her uncle's mission, the people he served. Again she felt that high resolve and quickening in her spirit that had made her determined to become a missionary, but she could not deny that she was looking forward to seeing Graham and John again.

"Perhaps my destiny here holds more than I realize."

Sunday services at Applegate Landing were held in the community church that doubled as a one-room school. A whitewashed building with the tiniest of bells in a miniature bell tower, it was removed from the main cluster of buildings, presumably to supply the worshipers and young scholars with some quiet for their prayers and studies.

Surprisingly to Gloriana, Graham Norton joined her and the Applegates as the small, high-pitched bell in the church steeple called Applegate Landing to worship. He fell into step beside her with a self-conscious grin that suggested he could read her thoughts and was perhaps as surprised as she.

"Sorry if I overstepped last night," he told her after a moment. "I guess I was just jealous. A pretty girl is an event in the life of a community like this one, and a girl like you is bound to cause a sensation."

Gloriana caught her breath and looked up at him to see if he were serious. A teasing smile lit the big man's features, softening the square jaw and transforming the blue eyes that could be so hard and menacing into sparkling messengers of mischief and fun. He had taken off his hat, letting the coppery curls fall boyishly across his forehead. And in place of his

40

savagely picturesque buckskins, he was wearing a simple dark suit. Yet the common attire emphasized, more than the frontier costume, the breadth of his shoulders, straining impressively against the rich broadcloth, and accentuated his towering height.

What a grand man! Gloriana thought to herself and then remembered too late as Graham laughed pleasantly that her family had always said that she had a transparent face, often articulating her thoughts better than words. To cover up her embarrassment, she began to chatter about why she had come to Oregon Territory, about her problem with the Missions Board, and her hopes for the future.

Again to her surprise, Graham listened sympathetically, and she was highly gratified when he laughed outright at the Mission Board's calling her a spinster.

Sunday services had always been a special time for Gloriana. In the spacious sanctuary of her father's church in Philadelphia, she had felt an inner soaring as the organ intoned the old hymns and the sunlight enhanced the jeweled pictures of the stained-glass windows. She had often wondered if the spiritual experience were intensified by the beauty of the surroundings. Yet in the little frontier school house with its bare board floors and a teacher's desk and a chalkboard where the altar and pulpit should be, God seemed as near, perhaps nearer.

The congregation sang unaccompanied and slightly off-key but with an enthusiasm that underscored their strong belief. The minister's message was as simple as the people themselves and reminded Gloriana of something her Uncle Ralph had written, "God is more real to us on the frontier because of our utter dependence on Him, every moment of the day."

Lord, help me to walk closer to You, she prayed earnestly. *Let me share the here-and-now faith of these people.* And with her head bowed, Gloriana felt a sudden premonition that she might soon need the Lord to strengthen and hide her, but just as surely came the assurance that when she needed Him, He would be there.

She had all but forgotten the freight master in the depths of her worship so that his voice startled her as they left the schoolhouse.

"You really believe in what old Reverend Samuels was talking about, don't you?"

"Why, yes, don't you?" Gloriana countered. She had assumed that because he went to church, she had misjudged Norton and he must be a Christian.

He waited a few minutes before answering, and his face looked more thoughtful, sad, and somehow vulnerable than she had ever seen it. "I don't know," he said finally, as much to himself as to her. "I don't know."

CHAPTER 5

SUNDAY AFTERNOON IN APPLEGATE LANDING was a social time. Neighbors dropped by to "sit a spell" on the Applegates' wide porch, and the sociable pioneer couple seemed tireless in their enthusiasm for their neighbors and for the frontier home they shared.

In the course of two hours Gloriana met the Jabbots, teenaged newlyweds whose beaming faces held no hint that their early marriage had come after a massacre left them the only remaining members of their respective families; Grandma Tuttle, who had raised two children and six grandchildren on the frontier, only to lose all but one in a typhoid epidemic the year before; Zack Humbard, the lone, fire-scarred survivor of the burning of the small mill town of Ashland by Rogue Indians. Every inhabitant of the little community, it seemed, came with a story, and Gloriana was astonished at the quiet heroism of these people who had suffered so much.

"Why do they stay?" she posed the question to her journal later that afternoon, and glancing up from her comfortable seat in the shade of a blooming trumpet

43

vine, she thought she could see the answer. Near at hand the Applegate yard was like any she might have been sitting in during a warm summer afternoon back home. But beyond the cultivated yard was an uncultivated paradise. To her right a gentle, sloping path lined with sunflowers, paintbrush, and the bright blue cornflowers that the pioneers called bachelor buttons climbed to a forested mountain. The dark stands of pine and fir seemed more inviting than forbidding, and the air was heavy with the spicy scents of pine, cedar, and juniper.

Just below the house the hillside gave way to a bluff that overhung a magnificent river, and to her left the community of Applegate Landing was a picturesque cluster of log buildings and square white cottages.

Gloriana had started to sketch the little community when a small moth the color of warm butter landed on her pencil. Its round body was covered with a soft, downy coat. Long antennae waved flirtatiously at her, and she had leaned forward to study the attractive little creature more closely when a voice just inches away startled her.

"Watch out! It might bite."

In spite of herself Gloriana jumped, and the harmless little creature took flight.

"Oh, how could you?" She looked up for a second into the disturbingly close face of Graham Norton and then let her eyes return regretfully to the retreating moth.

He laughed and stepped over the low porch rail to join her on the bench. He had changed from the conservative suit of the morning and was once again dressed in the trail buckskins that made him seem a bit savage and uncontrollable.

Graham had spent the early part of the afternoon preparing the freight wagons for the resumption of their journey the next day. He would be taking most of the wagons on south to the gold fields at Jacksonville, he told her, but he had arranged for her own wagons to move east to Klamath Mission under the protection of the cavalry troop.

"I have no choice but to go on with the main part of the wagon train. But you'll be safe. I'm sending you with the soldiers. And I've detailed some of my best teamsters to drive your wagons. Jones, Blackjack, and Smitty will take care of everything," he assured her. The three teamsters, Gloriana noted, were some of those she had known and liked best on the trip from Crescent City.

With the arrangements for the next day's journey made, an uncomfortable silence fell between the two. Gloriana, faced with the realization that she might not be seeing this infuriating but strangely intriguing man again, wanted to ask him if he ever visited her uncle's mission. But Graham, intent on some brooding thought whose secret was hidden somewhere in the valley mists, seemed remote and unapproachable.

She was about to make a lame excuse about needing her rest and escape the silence by retreating inside the house when Graham suddenly grasped her hand and pulled her to her feet.

"Come with me," he said, taking her hand and starting toward the forest pathway.

The pathway was the same one, climbing through tangles of wildflowers to the lush tree forest, that Gloriana had found so appealing earlier. What she had not noticed before was that it was a rather lonely and secluded path, hidden from the community by the bulk of the Applegate house and by a stand of jack pines.

She tried not to dwell on the impropriety of being alone in the forest with a young man, but she pulled her hand away from his grasp, then wished she had not as the trail proved to be rougher than it appeared from a distance.

"Where are we going?" Gloriana asked after a few minutes of scrambling up the hillside.

45

"Blessing Waters. It's just a ways further," Graham answered imperturbably, taking hold of her arm to steer her toward the trees. Gloriana hesitated, remembering that she did not know this man well and that she was in the West where standards of behavior were decidedly more liberal than what she was accustomed to in the East. But the cool shadows beckoned, and soon she found herself gliding between massive tree trunks on a thick, springy carpet of pine needles.

Graham's earlier dark mood had dissipated, and he was at his best, showing her how to read directions in the forest by looking for the spidery green moss growing on the north sides of the tree trunks or where to find fragrant mountain lilies in the dense sheltering growth around fallen logs.

"How long have you been in the West? How do you know all of these things?" Gloriana asked him.

"I came in '39," he told her, "before there were any trails. And I know most of what I know because of the Klamaths. I lived among them for several years after my parents died." He said no more, and Gloriana did not press him further, but the confidence revealed another side of the man, one more vulnerable and more feeling than the tough wagon boss usually exposed to view.

Blessing Waters proved to be an icy cold spring in a glade so well-hidden and beautiful it seemed a dream. The water bubbled up from the base of a black rock thick with moss and lichens to spill into a little stone basin at its base. Charged with some kind of gas deep beneath the earth, the waters frothed mysteriously, and a white crust of mineral deposits had formed around the edge of the pool.

"Make a cup of your hand like this." Graham showed Gloriana how to squeeze and curve her fingers so that they would hold the water. Then he knelt down in the grass at the edge of the pool and proceeded to scoop up the sparkling liquid.

Feeling self-conscious but determined to be a good sport, Gloriana followed suit. At first the water dribbled quickly between her fingers, but after a few tries she managed to hold enough to take a few sips.

"Why, it's delicious! Tangy and kind of salty as though there were minerals in it."

"The Indians say it's blessed by the spirits," Graham told her in the quiet voice, almost a whisper, the hushed glade seemed to call for. An almost perfect circle of blue-green colored firs—silvertips, Graham called them— enclosed them in a magic ring. The usual forest sounds of birds' calling and animals' rustling through the undergrowth were muffled by the music of the spring. The forest-scented air was still and so spiced with cedar and pine that it stung the lungs to breathe deeply.

"Is all of this natural?" Gloriana asked, feeling the softness of the grass carpet they were sitting on. "I mean, did someone plant the trees so they would grow that way? And who keeps the grass so short, almost like a lawn?"

"Probably the deer come here at night to graze. Maybe some enterprising brave planted the trees."

"You mean sort of like a shrine to honor the spirits?"

"More likely to have some privacy with his sweetheart."

Something in Graham's tone as well as his words made Gloriana suddenly aware of how alone they were and how close. She moved her arm, and it brushed against Graham's sleeve, sending something like a lightning bolt through her. Glancing up, she found his face close and a disturbing light in the depths of those sea-blue eyes.

"It's getting late. We had better go," she said hastily and started to rise, but he held her back with a strong arm that enveloped her gently, but firmly.

"Not quite yet," he said, still speaking quietly and

moving nearer. His free hand came up to trace the soft outline of her lips and wipe away a stray drop of the blessing water.

"This is outrageous. I insist you release me immediately."

She had no time to protest further before Graham's searching lips found hers, and Gloriana found herself picked up and cradled as though she were no larger than a child. For an awful instant she felt something inside of her, thrilling to Graham's kiss, willing her to return it, to let the growing force of his passion carry both of them along to some unknown realm. Pressed against him, she felt her own body yielding, molding against the hardness and strength of his. Then the realization of what was happening shot through her, numbing her senses and lending her the power to wrench herself free of his embrace.

"Glory, wait! You don't understand." Graham started after her, but the speechless fury he read in Gloriana's face said she would not, could not listen.

The Applegate table had an uncharacteristic lack of company that evening. The meal began silently with Gloriana deep in her own thoughts and the Applegates at a loss as to how to entertain their suddenly moody guest.

"I understand you took a walk to the Blessing Waters," Cynthia Ann said at last when several attempts at introducing a suitable topic for conversation had failed. "It's a magic spring, you know. Legend has it that if a man and a woman kneel together to drink at the spring, their love will be blessed and their union eternal, extending even past the grave to the stars. Isn't that a lovely notion?"

She was totally unprepared for Gloriana's stricken expression or for the quick tears that leaped to her eyes, sending her with hasty, choked excuses from the table.

"Why, whatever did I say?" the bewildered lady asked her husband.

"I'm afraid that for once the blessing of the waters didn't take very well," Jesse Applegate, who had witnessed the young couple's abrupt departure for the spring and equally abrupt return, replied enigmatically.

Upstairs in her bed Gloriana shed quick tears of shame, until she lay still as questions shot through her mind. Why had Graham Norton tricked her into the blessing ritual of kneeling together and drinking from the spring? Had he known about the ritual? He must have. He knew all the legends and stories about this place. Why hadn't he said anything? But wait! Hadn't he called her back, wanting to explain? Why hadn't she waited? Would she ever know what he wanted to say?

It was past midnight before she remembered to seek help from the only unfailing Source.

Lord, help me deal with this, she prayed quietly. From deep inside her came the question of a still, small voice: *What would you have done if this young man had declared his love for you? Would you have accepted him, knowing, as he told you this morning, that he does not share your faith?*

A truthful answer was the only possible one. "I would have had to say no," she admitted at last.

Then how much better it was that he did not ask, that whatever may or may not be between you was left for God's will and the future to work out.

Tear stains still on her cheeks, Gloriana slept with renewed peace, assured that once again "all things had worked together for good" and that her future held more excitement and promise than she had dreamed when she left home to be a missionary.

CHAPTER 6

LEAVING APPLEGATE LANDING was like leaving home. Gloriana looked back regretfully as her wagon crept farther and farther down the valley. A light fog, rolling off the river, wrapped the just-waking community in a filmy white haze, giving it a dream-like appearance. The mist obscured the southbound wagon route, but she could imagine the heavily loaded wagons of Graham Norton's train moving slowly up river toward the place they called Jacksonville.

Graham had checked her wagons carefully and watched them start. His expression had been carefully noncommittal as he hurried from place to place, giving orders and testing the loads to see if they had been securely packed, giving special attention and adding an extra rope to hold the organ. But before they had started, he had come to stand beside Gloriana, his hat in his hand, seemingly having something to say but not knowing how to say it.

Finally, he asked her to tell her uncle that he would be at the mission in two months to do some work they had apparently agreed upon. Then warning Gloriana once again to watch her step with Lieutenant Tilton, he had ordered the teamsters to start the wagons.

Graham had also had a few words with John Tilton—not very pleasant words, it seemed, from the scowl on the lieutenant's face. Gloriana imagined she knew the gist of what was said from her own driver's repeated assurances that he would be "lookin' out fer her, extry special."

Her driver was Smitty, her favorite of all the teamsters, for he combined a fine sense of humor with a highly developed love for conversation, something Gloriana had learned to appreciate when she had ridden with one close-mouthed driver on the trip from Crescent City. Yet even Smitty took a while to warm up and, during the early hours at least, Gloriana found herself alone with her thoughts.

They were not unpleasant. She recalled joyfully the new friends she had made—the villagers who had welcomed her so uncritically; the admiring young farmers; the Applegates, who had assured her they would look for her to come for a long visit in the spring. The episode of Blessing Waters and Graham Norton was one thing she studiously avoided; she found an odd gratification in knowing that the matter would be there to consider when she chose. Moreover, the frontiersman himself might be planning to take up where they had left off when he visited the mission in just two short months.

In the meantime she was on the last leg of her journey, and the excitement was mounting at the prospect of seeing her beloved uncle and beginning the work she had come so far to do.

It would take four days to climb the remaining mountain range, Smitty told her when he finally emerged from his own private early morning fog— perhaps the result of a long Sunday night in the village tavern, rather than the dampening effect of the river mist.

"We c'ld make it a mile shorter if we went by the Greensprings," the man confided what appeared to have been a disagreement with his boss, "but all things rightly consider'd, yu bein' a female 'n all, this here root may be the best'un."

The route they were taking was called the Dead Indian Pass, and Gloriana shuddered a bit at the implications of the name. Still the soldiers did not seem unduly concerned, so she supposed they were not in any real danger. Lieutenant Tilton himself found ample opportunity to ride alongside Gloriana's wagon. She had no doubt that if it had not been for Smitty's inhospitable glowering, the lieutenant would have forsaken his horse for a bumpy four-day ride on the hard wagon seat.

"I wouldn't be payin' no mind to that un's jawin'," Smitty told her with a curt nod of his bushy head in the lieutenant's direction. "There's sum thet only means t'alf o' what they say and less'n thet o' what they look."

"Now, Smitty, you are going to have to back that up with something more substantial," Gloriana tried to pump the driver for more information. "What is it you and Mr. Norton have against Lieutenant Tilton? Do you know something about him? If there is something I should know, I want you to tell me. Otherwise, I have no choice but to think you are entertaining some ill-natured grudge against the man."

But for once the talkative Smitty would say nothing, and in fact, his offended silence stretched into several hours and only began to thaw when Gloriana made a sketch in her journal of a grumpy bear driving a freight wagon while a timid girl peeked nervously over the wagon seat behind him.

"Don't draw me unless you make me a dashing knight on a prancing horse," John Tilton said when he saw her handiwork, "or maybe a cavalier in a long, flowing cape, climbing the balcony to woo the beautiful lady."

"I could as easily make you a savage chief in warpaint on a wild Indian pony," Gloriana countered his extravagance with some of her own, but she could tell by the expression on the lieutenant's face that he did not like the idea and she dropped it. *What absurd vanity,* she commented to herself, determined not to draw someone who had such a high opinion of himself that he had to play only the roles he chose even in someone else's fantasies.

The Dead Indian Pass was as rugged as any they had passed through. The wagons crept slowly along a trail at times barely discernible in the hard, rocky canyon floors. Several times they had to unhitch the mules and use block and tackle to get the wagons down a sharp incline or across a deep gully. Once or twice Gloriana was certain her precious organ had reached the end of its eventful journey, but each time Graham Norton's teamsters managed to save it.

The soldiers, Gloriana noticed, including the tirelessly gallant lieutenant, were less helpful. In fact, she had the distinct impression that if it had not been for their leader's interest in her, they might very well have moved on about their business, leaving the slow-moving wagons to make their own way, unescorted. With every mile she appreciated more her sturdy drivers and the careful watch they mounted over her.

The first night's camp was made in a wildly beautiful spot with the unprepossessing name of Lake of the Woods. A perfect gem of blue in the late afternoon, the lake turned to a silvery mirror at evening, reflecting an enormous yellow moon. Sitting by a fire built especially by Smitty for her bedside, Gloriana marveled at the brightness of the moonlight magnified in the mirror of the lake.

She had leaned back against the trunk of a tree, her eyes closed, her thoughts straying again to the two days at Applegate Landing, when a faint cracking sound, like boots' stepping quietly over mats of dry pine needles brought her upright in time to see John Tilton step out of the darkness.

"Did I startle you?" he asked, his speech seeming a bit slurred to Gloriana's heightened senses. "I couldn't sleep and thought you might like to go for a walk down by the lake." His words were casual enough, but in the darkness he seemed to be staring at her with a peculiar intensity.

"I was just getting ready to retire," Gloriana excused herself hastily. "It has been a long ride, and tomorrow will be even longer."

"All right," he seemed to accept her decision easily enough. Still, he did not leave but crouched down on a branch of the fallen tree that screened Gloriana's bed from the others and began talking about the lake and moonlight in a oddly thick voice, struggling, it seemed, over the pronunciation of some words and sliding over others.

"Lieutenant, I would really like to get some sleep," she told him pointedly, assuming her most authoritative tone.

He stood up, but instead of starting back toward the men's camp, he took another step in her direction. What would have happened she was thankfully never to know, for at that moment the underbrush erupted with crackling and snapping and Blackjack stepped out of the bushes with an enormous load of firewood in his arms.

"Enough wood to keep it burning all night," he told her cheerfully, not seeming to see the lieutenant. Then he took an enormous gun out of his belt and handed it to her. "I almost forgot that Graham said to give you this to keep close by to guard against skunks and other varmints."

Gloriana accepted the gun thankfully. She had never liked guns or known what to do with them, but this one gave her at least the look of meaning business.

Blackjack took his time stacking the wood close by her bedroll where she could easily reach it to pile on the fire. Then he added a few sticks to the flames. By the time he had finished, the lieutenant was gone.

The three days that followed were as tense as any Gloriana had experienced. Her three drivers rode on guard, their usually jovial attitudes submerged in a grim watchfulness that included the soldiers as well as the forests in its scope. After the second day, when Gloriana had half-expected to awake to find the cavalry gone, she decided that nothing more unusual had happened than that the lieutenant had had too much to drink and had become unfortunately amorous.

Lieutenant Tilton acted as though nothing had happened, which of course was literally the case. If he felt any embarrassment for the episode, he did not show it. Perhaps he did not even remember. Gloriana had known patients at the hospital where she had worked in Philadelphia who could not remember entire weeks during which they had been drinking heavily.

In any case, she thought it best to go on in the old way, smiling at the young man's constant sallies and seeming to enjoy his flirting. She had an idea that it would not be wise to alienate this mysterious young man. And when she caught him in an unguarded moment looking at the driver Blackjack, something dark and menacing in his expression confirmed her suspicion and caused her to wonder how much was hidden behind the handsome, laughing face of Lieutenant John Tilton.

Dead Indian Pass   August 27, 1851
    We camped today on the cone of a volcano. Mount McLoughlin has a spectacular beauty like no mountain I

55

have ever seen before. It rises abruptly from the rolling, forested hills and soars upward until its rounded peak is lost in the clouds. The trees seem to grow taller and lusher in the thick gray volcanic ash on its sides and the rounded cone of the mountain is ribboned with enchanting, lacy waterfalls as the edges of a white snow cap, still deep in spite of the August heat, melt.

Yet for all its beauty, I cannot help thinking of the enormous destructive power lying just out of sight, perhaps building unseen beneath the surface of the mountain.

The Indians, I am told, call these ethereally lovely peaks devil mountains. I appreciate the comparison and will be glad when we break camp in the morning.

"Miss Windemere, I think you would enjoy seeing Bridal Veil Falls. Would you care to accompany me?"

Gloriana looked over her shoulder into the smiling face of John Tilton, close enough to have been reading her journal. She felt a moment's relief that she had not been writing anything about him. Something in the man's eyes put her thought of pleading fatigue aside. She and her little wagon train were still dependent on his protection. Forcing a bright smile of assent, Gloriana let the man help her to her feet and was relieved to see that the indefinable something had vanished from his expression, letting the smile on his lips touch his eyes.

"You can hear the falls from here," he told her, showing a marked tendency to hold onto her hand rather than release it. "But nearby the rocks pick up the music, and it sounds like a chorus of water nymphs."

"How is it that something as temporary as a waterfall caused by the melting snow has earned a name?" Gloriana asked brightly, trying not to see the disapproving looks which her drivers—Jones, Blackjack, and Smitty— threw in her direction.

"This one isn't temporary," the lieutenant laughed as she managed to extract her hand; he offered his arm instead with all the aplomb of a ballroom gallant. "It starts in a hot spring near the summit. The warm water melts the snow whatever the time of year, though in the summer the falls sometimes expand to a broad curtain across the face of the rock." Was it her imagination, or did the man send a sly grin in the direction of Graham Norton's teamsters as he tucked the hand that she had placed lightly on his sleeve securely into the crook of his arm?

Gloriana was surprised to find a path leading to the falls. "Could that many people have found this place?" she asked Tilton.

"The path is a deer trail. If we move quietly, we may see a doe or two. The bucks are usually more cautious."

Peering into the shadows made by the sinking sun and the tall trees, Gloriana imagined she could feel the deer close by, their great liquid brown eyes following her curiously.

As they neared the falls, the simple tune of the water expanded to a water fugue as the echoes multiplied the sounds. But nothing had prepared Gloriana for the witchery of the falls. Tumbling from a rocky cliff nearly a thousand feet above, the white, splashing water made a lacy curtain hundreds of feet across, then billowed high in the air at the base. It looked indeed like a bridal veil falling into a long, frothy train.

Spellbound, Gloriana couldn't speak, but after a moment she realized that her companion's eyes were on her face and not the falls. She felt a tension in the air and sensed the volatile depths of this man, held in check just beneath the surface.

They were several yards back down the deer trail before the falls' wild ecstasy of sound subsided enough for voices to be heard. What the lieutenant said surprised Gloriana no less than the careful courtesy of his touch as he helped her across a tiny rivulet of water that appeared suddenly in the trail.

57

"I beg your pardon for frightening you the other night. I am afraid sometimes it takes a beautiful, cultivated woman to remind us what brutes this wilderness can make of men. I hope you can forgive me and allow us to be friends." He stopped in the trail and held out his hand in the manly gesture of friendship.

"I'm happy . . . that is, of course we can be friends," Gloriana faltered and held out her small hand to be captured in his large one.

"And I hope you will allow me to see you when you are busy spreading salvation among the poor red devils," he continued in the old teasing way. "We white devils could use some saving too."

Gloriana had no idea what she answered, but she had a distinct impression of Graham Norton's scowling at her from somewhere as she smiled tentatively at the handsome cavalry officer and allowed him to take her arm as they followed the lengthening shadows slowly back to camp.

CHAPTER 7

NEVER WOULD GLORIANA FORGET her first glimpse of
Klamath Mission. Her wagons and their escort had
emerged from the trees at the end of a hazardous
morning's travel to find themselves on the edge of a
fresh-water lake so large it seemed almost like an
inland sea. Then she had seen it—a small cluster of
buildings under massive willow trees. And stretching
for acres and acres around the buildings were little
huts that looked as though they had been made from
sticks and animal skins.

"But I don't understand! That looks like an entire
Indian village. I thought my uncle had only a few
natives staying at the mission."

"Perhaps there's a celebration," Tilton said.
"Sometimes the natives gather for a pow wow—a
kind of religious get-together with singing and dancing
to honor their gods." Why the Indians would be
holding a celebration for a native religion at a
Christian mission, the lieutenant didn't hazard a
guess, and Gloriana received the impression that the
man neither knew nor cared much about the Klamath
Lake Medical Mission.

Their coming was greeted by a few black-haired children who ran to meet the wagons, but for the most part the faces that watched their progress through the Indian encampment were guarded and expressionless.

"Cap'n, these reddies ain't lookin' none too friendly," Gloriana thought she heard one of Tilton's men call to him, but she realized she was mistaken since Tilton's rank was lieutenant, not captain.

Uncle Ralph was standing on the porch of the largest cabin—a long, low building of peeled, whitewashed logs, which Gloriana immediately realized was the hospital. Smiles wreathed the cherubic face with its little fluff of white whiskers and wisps of white hair winging out above round ears. But she read weariness and relief in the welcome as well as gladness to see his niece, and the doctor's attention turned quickly to the wagons of supplies.

She explained their loss quickly but had not finished her inventory of items taken before Smitty stepped forward and said in a low voice, "Ma'am, Graham and old Jesse Applegate made up most of yer losses with supplies at the Landing before we left. They reckoned as how it'd be a mite easier for them to bring up more from San Francisky th'n fer you'all to git more, bein' off the beaten track 'n all."

The boxes of camphorated oil were especially valued, and when he had assured himself of an ample supply, Uncle Ralph explained that there was a measles epidemic, and the oil helped sooth the rash on the children's sensitive skin.

Gloriana paled as she recalled what a measles epidemic meant among the native peoples. She had nursed in several epidemics in Philadelphia, and always the disease had claimed more than its share of victims. For the Indians, whose immune systems were less developed, even the milder strains of the illness could prove fatal. She had heard of entire tribes' being wiped out before the epidemic had run its course.

In the midst of such an emergency there was little time to deliver all the messages from back home or to dwell on the delight of being on the mission field at last or even to say goodbye to the companions of her journey from Applegate Landing. Gloriana had a glimpse of a small whitewashed room with shutters instead of glass windows where Uncle Ralph directed the teamsters to put her trunks and boxes. She met the staff as they worked—a second doctor, Eugene Midfield, a young man just out of medical school and his wife of a year, who during the emergency had taken on the task of cooking for the staff. Matilda (Tildy) Brown, her uncle's housekeeper, Gloriana already knew. Tildy's sturdy hands and loud voice were busily managing the outdoor washroom. From steaming cauldrons she covered a labyrinth of clotheslines with clean sheets, rags, and an assortment of shirts and missionary-barrel garments that were serving as hospital gowns.

"The hospital was filled long ago; now we'll need to set up a children's ward in the schoolhouse," Uncle Ralph told her. He introduced her to Oweena, a Shasta girl who said she had contracted and recovered from the illness years before when she had lived in the white man's settlement of Eureka on the coast. Together the young women set about clearing the long schoolroom of its makeshift desks and scouring the bare wood floor, where for want of beds or pallets they would lay their charges.

It was past midnight when Gloriana found her way to the kitchen of her uncle's cabin for a bite of supper. She was surprised to find the teamsters there and even more surprised to find that Jones, Blackjack, and Smitty were leaving the mission. "We're gittin' while the gittin's good," was all Jones said, but Smitty confided that they would return by the Greensprings, the route he had preferred all along.

"Hsst! Ye needn't tell everythin' ye know," the

usually silent Jones interjected with a quick look around the empty kitchen with its still hot iron range and the split-log table and benches, as though he were looking for some invisible enemy.

Mystified, Gloriana said a silent prayer for the men. Perhaps there were hostile Indians in the mission camp that Uncle Ralph did not know about—although what he could do if he could tell the dangerous from the nondangerous she had no idea. Minutes later, just slipping off to sleep, she heard the wagons roll by her window; the usual clip-clopping of the mules' hooves sounded muffled as though they had been bound with something soft, and someone must have greased the squeaky wheel on the wagon that had carried the organ, for she could no longer hear its agonized, nerve-shattering whine.

She woke a few hours later to a timid knock on her door and a sense of urgency.

"Miss Glory, Dr. Ralph says we should hurry to be ready for the sick ones by chapel time." Having no idea how chapel time and her patients were related, Gloriana nonetheless followed Oweena's advice and hurried. But she took the time to find and don one of her hospital uniforms. The gray-striped gown with its heavy gray wrap-around apron made her feel thoroughly the nurse once again, and her assistant's covertly admiring glance made her determine to cut down one of the uniforms to fit the Shasta girl at the first opportunity.

It was a little past dawn, and the wonderful lake smells of clean water and wet tules filled the air. Overhead, gulls were winging across the blue waves, intent on a breakfast of fish. Their ragged calling reminded Gloriana of the months at sea, and, in spite of the grim atmosphere hanging over the epidemic camp, she felt a deep thankfulness to be at the mission and about the work she had chosen.

"You have come just in time," Uncle Ralph told her over a quick breakfast of some bland cooked grains that she was too tense to want but too experienced to refuse. She forced Oweena to eat a small bowl too and urged some as well on the sweet-faced cook. Mrs. Midfield refused with a wan smile and a movement of her hand to her stomach. Noticing the slight fulness of the woman's gown, Gloriana guessed morning sickness and hoped that it was not a German measles epidemic they were dealing with.

"Isn't it still early to be experiencing an epidemic of this type?" Gloriana asked, remembering that back home the summer months were the time to worry about typhoid but rarely measles.

"I usually expect something like this in the spring," was her uncle's frowning reply. "Coming now could mean we will have a short siege; let's pray it's not the direct opposite." Then he gave Gloriana instructions about the ages of children he wanted her to house in the ward, the treatment he was using, and the arrangements for sanitation. He repeated Oweena's enigmatic statement about finding her patients at chapel, but again she let it pass without questioning. She would find out what was meant soon enough.

Unlike Applegate Landing, the mission could boast a schoolhouse separate from its church. Set away from the other buildings, it was perched atop a grassy hill where the lake mists would be dispelled rather than linger in the mornings. Two outhouses separated by some bushes were hidden behind the hill. "Too far for the sick ones to travel," Gloriana noticed with concern and wondered if she and Oweena would be able to handle everything alone.

During the night someone had spread the clean floors with comfortable looking beds of animal skins.

"My people give their own sleeping rugs," Oweena told her proudly. Gloriana did not have the heart to tell her that the rugs could be infected. Besides, she knew that she would need some kind of bedding in addition to the assortment of makeshift sheets and quilts she had already taken from the main hospital for the sick babies to lie on. Still she would make her ward as safe as she could, and mixing some disinfectant with water in a wooden bucket, Gloriana went about sprinkling the skins, all the while praying that they would dry before she had to put patients on them.

Chapel bells—a miscellaneous but not unmelodious assortment of dinner gongs and cow bells strung on a tripod beside the church door—sounded at nine o'clock. To Gloriana's amazement the entire encampment, sick and well alike, responded to the summons.

"They come for big medicine," Oweena told her, and Gloriana realized that this was the reason she was to choose her patients at chapel. To the Indians the service with its singing and prayers must be a major part of the healing ritual, more akin to the practices of their own medicine men than the unfamiliar hospital regimen of medicines and constant sterilizing.

The short message that morning was presented by Dr. Midfield, standing on the elevated porch and speaking to the Indians gathered in the church yard since the building itself could not hold so many. If she had not been so busy scanning the crowd for the teary eyes and coughs and the painful itching that would signal measles rash, Gloriana would have been fascinated by the manner of the service.

Some of the Indians at least were not new to Christian worship, for they sang what appeared to be simple Sunday-school choruses readily enough. The words were a mixture of English and Klamath, the language most spoken by the various tribes that had assembled. But the half-chanted music, punctuated by drumbeats was entirely native, bearing little resemblance to the melodic lines and careful harmonies intended by the songwriters.

The sermon itself was more visual than oral, although Midfield spoke in what sounded like an Indian language and there were several interpreters posted around him, all, it seemed, talking at the same time. Several mission Indians, their status indicated by their mission-barrel dress rather than native costumes, held up a twenty-foot long sheet, the different segments of which had been carefully stitched together to show a long mural of brightly painted illustrations. Gloriana had heard of the Catholic Ladder; a kind of scale marking important events in religious history from creation to the coming of Christ and the present missionary movements, it had been used by the priests to give the Indians a sense of perspective and the progression of Church history. She had even seen a copy of the Protestant Ladder, a similar scale with an added dimension to show the differences between Catholic and Protestant theology. Whoever had made the Klamath Mission Ladder seemed to be more interested in presenting an illustrated Bible than in either church history or controversies. The success of the little cluster of pictures representing each familiar story could best be gauged by the eagerness with which the Indians pressed forward to get a closer look as Dr. Midfield pointed to the part of the sheet that illustrated his sermon.

His story was Daniel in the Lion's Den—an odd choice, Gloriana thought, for a sick camp. She would have chosen the loaves and fishes or Christ and the lepers, but the crowd seemed impressed. Perhaps the timid-looking Dr. Midfield felt exactly like Daniel in the midst of so many desperate and not fully comprehending natives. She remembered that one reason given in the Eastern papers for the killing of the Whitmans was that they had let too many of the Cayuse people die in epidemics just like this one.

The sad, feverish faces of the children and the anxious, frightened faces of the Indian mothers wrung

Gloriana's heart. They came to her reluctantly but obediently after the service. With some a quick look at the vivid red rash on arms and chests established the presence of the disease. With others she found the first hectic blotches behind the ears or discovered tiny red Koplik's spots in their mouths. After more than an hour of examinations, she had selected thirty, choosing those with the worst rashes or a deep cough that threatened the dreaded complication of pneumonia.

Dozens of others showed various stages of the disease—teary eyes, fever, a rash just starting at the hairline, or the welcome sloughing off of the skin that indicated that the measles had nearly run its course. In these cases she told the mothers through Oweena to keep the children's eyes shaded and give them fluids but no solid foods—all the while unsure whether there was much milk available in the crowded camp or whether the Indians were in the habit of cooking nourishing soups.

The schoolhouse was soon filled to its limit, but unlike the crying, cranky patients of most children's wards Gloriana had worked in, these were quiet. Their suffering showed only in the dark eyes that followed her as she moved from child to child, spooning liquids into their mouths or dabbing angry blotches with camphorated oil.

Oweena soon recruited two more Indian girls to help, and Gloriana was relieved to learn that they also had survived the "red sickness." The Indian girl was a Godsend, never tiring, always moving quickly and, even before she was asked, coming to explain a procedure to a frightened patient or to help pry open the clenched teeth of a stubborn one.

Usually Gloriana eased her way around a children's ward with smiles and teasing, but her overtures here met only with blank expressions. Thinking she must seem too alien and forbidding, she asked Oweena to teach her some expressions in the Klamath language.

66

Then after rehearsing the words several times, she confidently approached a girl of about six and spoke the words Oweena had said meant, "Open your mouth." The reaction was electrifying as the girl's face broke into a broad grin and the patients close by all joined in the rhythmic, sing-song laugh typical of the Indians.

Glad to see the smiles but mystified as to the reason, Gloriana turned to her assistant only to find the girl laughing silently behind her.

"Oweena, what did I say to this child?"

"Oh, Miss Glory, you say okay; you just say so fun-nee."

Gloriana supposed her pronunciation could be that atrocious, but she still could not help looking suspiciously at the Shasta girl's wide-eyed, innocent face and made up her mind to check out her newly learned phrases with the mission staff before she used them on any other patients.

At least she had broken the ice. Now Oweena and the other girls went around the room teasing in the Indian way, which seemed to consist in part of poking and pinching and pulling braids. Gloriana herself seemed to be a primary source of amusement and little brown-cheeked cherubs giggled behind their hands as she approached them.

Uncle Ralph checked her ward late in the afternoon, and his tired face brightened considerably at the air of good feeling and the willingness with which the sick children were submitting to the nursing.

"I wish we could have you work some of this magic in the main hospital," he told her with a smile that could not altogether erase the worry in his face.

"I'm afraid the magic is Oweena's." And she told him about her attempt at communication.

"Well, my dear, we all have our own methods," he broke into a hearty laugh that set the ward giggling again. "You told the child you were Sky Woman and had come to bite off her nose."

CHAPTER 8

Long hours of patient nursing stretched into days and finally into weeks. The makeshift beds in Gloriana's children's hospital yielded up their occupants—some to return to their families, alive and whole again, some to occupy freshly dug graves in the growing cemetary by the lakeside.

And still there were more sufferers to take their places.

In the third week of September the golden Oregon summer changed into wet, misty fall. Rain fell in a slow, steady drizzle that soaked the grasslands around the mission. The waters of the lake rose inch by inch, and a damp cloud seemed to have settled over the mission.

Among the sick the wetness intensified the danger of pneumonia. Day and night the fires burned in the hospital and the schoolhouse, but though the heavy iron stoves repeatedly came close to overheating, they could not keep out the dampness.

"Miss Glory, I think your God must not like Indians very much," Oweena told her late one night.

Gloriana sent a quick prayer for wisdom winging heavenward, then answered earnestly, "He not only likes you; He loves you so much that He sent His Son to die for you."

"Then why do we suffer so much?"

There it was—the age-old question and one that had often bothered Gloriana. "All I know, Oweena, is that our suffering hurts Him very much and that He has promised a time will come when there will be no more suffering. In the meantime we must do all we can to help each other bear whatever comes. That's why we missionaries are here—to help your people through times of sickness like this one."

The Shasta girl said nothing more, but the thoughtfulness of her expression made Gloriana hope she had said something to touch the girl's heart.

The days of the epidemic had taken their toll on the mission's resources as well as on its people. The medical supplies Gloriana had brought were nearly gone. Even food was running low as the Klamath hunters fell victim one after another to the measles. And with the cold and the need for fires, the mission woodpiles, so laboriously stockpiled in anticipation of the harsh Oregon winters, were disappearing quickly.

Knowing that the army had sent Lieutenant Tilton and his company to build a fort somewhere in the south, Gloriana suggested her uncle send a runner to ask for the army's help. "When there was a typhoid epidemic in Philadelphia, the government sent the guards to help," she remembered. She did not say that perhaps the lieutenant might come for *her* sake, if not the mission's.

Ralph Windemere walked to the door of his hospital office and, swinging it open, watched the steady downpour of rain. The moisture seemed to have washed the color from the landscape and left a gray, fluid world in which the division between sky and earth had blurred and finally run together.

"You must understand, my dear," he told her at last. "I have no doubt that in the East the authorities would be most helpful in a situation like this, but here things are different." He took his pipe from his pocket and clenched it between his teeth, but he didn't try to light it—probably, Gloriana guessed, he had shared his tobacco with some of his patients and had none left.

"Still, if you think it is worth a try, I will send someone to talk to this Lieutenant Tilton of yours."

Gloriana felt herself blushing and protested that he was not her lieutenant, but the truth was that she had been counting on his feelings for her being at least deep enough for him to want to please her. Certainly the young man had shown little concern for the missionaries. *If Graham Norton were here, he would help*. The thought came unbidden, and Gloriana suddenly remembered that in all those weeks she had not delivered the man's message.

"Now that is good news!" Ralph Windemere exclaimed as she haltingly told him what Graham Norton had promised. "Norton is a man who gets things done. We will need him badly when this is over." He paused a moment, then glancing curiously at his red-faced niece, added, "I take it you got to know the man rather well."

"We were on the freight train together from Crescent City—that is, I hired him to bring our supplies from the coast." For a moment Gloriana felt oddly transparent as though her perceptive uncle were looking directly inside her. His chuckle increased the feeling, and she noticed that he had reached in his pocket and was beginning again the ritual of the empty pipe.

"If I may ask, what did you think of this Western giant?" her uncle asked with that teasing tone Gloriana found more annoying in direct proportion to the degree of truth in the insinuations.

70

For a moment she did not answer. What exactly did she think of Graham Norton? Then, eyes flashing, she said, "If you must know, uncle, I found him vain, overbearing, and . . . insufferable!"

Ralph Windemere's beaming face fell a bit before his niece's apparent anger. "Why, child, I have known Graham Norton for nearly two years, and I have always found him to be kind and generous to a fault. Certainly, he takes charge, but this is the West. It takes strong men to survive. Did you know that his folks were missionaries? They were killed, not by Indians, but by white renegades when Norton was about sixteen. A Klamath chief took him in and treated him like a son—like an Indian prince."

Gloriana listened, fascinated, feeling a sudden rush of compassion for the man but also a little thrill of excitement. She could well imagine Graham as an arrogant native prince—daring anyone to defy him. No wonder he was accustomed to having his own way in everything and no wonder he knew the Indian rituals so well, including the romantic ceremonies of the Blessing Waters.

Lost and unconscious in her thoughts, Gloriana did not see the satisfied smile return to her uncle's face.

The first day of October passed, and still no help had come. Dr. Midfield had taken several of the convalescent men and gone to the nearby forests for wood. The unaccustomed work had resulted in a mass of blisters on his sensitive hands. Moreover, the wood had proved to be so damp that it smoked badly when they burned it.

Klamath Mission   October 3, 1851
  We watch the trails daily for signs of help's coming, yet I am the only one who seems to expect any relief from the army. Uncle Ralph talks hopefully of Graham Norton's promised arrival. Dr. Midfield continues to organize convalescents for hunting and wood chopping parties, but his accomplishments are meager.

In the midst of all our anxieties, my friend and helper Oweena seems to have bloomed mysteriously. She confided in me that help is on the way, and at first I thought she shared my faith in the army's willingness to meet our needs, but now I think she has some other, secret hope that she is not ready to reveal.

The army did come. It was a little after nine o'clock and chapel, still attended faithfully in spite of the storm and the crowded conditions in the small church, had just begun. The organ, which Gloriana had guarded so faithfully through the thousands of miles of travel, had been enthroned on a slightly elevated platform at the front of the church. Gloriana, pumping carefully, for the dampness made the organ notes unpredictable, was playing "A Mighty Fortress Is Our God" when a small boy rushed in with the news that soldiers were coming. A ripple of something like fear went through the congregation, and Gloriana thought she saw a few of the younger men slip out the door. But she breathed a deep prayer of thankfulness.

"Well, my dear, it seems you were right after all," Dr. Windemere told Gloriana.

"I just knew they would answer our appeal if only we had the faith," she answered joyfully, not stopping to think that her words were a criticism of her long-suffering uncle.

But her joy was soon tempered. Instead of the full company of men and the train of supply wagons she had expected, there were three soldiers leading two pack mules, neither very heavily laden. The men did not dismount; the expressions on their faces were guarded and strained, and Gloriana remembered the master sergeant's comment about unfriendly "red-dies" when the soldiers had escorted her to the mission in September.

The same sergeant was leading this expedition. When he recognized Gloriana, he stepped forward and handed her a thick packet and inquired after Dr. Windemere for whom he had a smaller envelope.

"Lieutenant Tilton sends his compliments, ma'am," the sergeant told Gloriana briefly. Then he asked where to unload the supplies.

Those supplies included barely enough cornmeal and jerked venison to feed the convalescent patients for a day or two. The bulk of the load was made up of coffee, tea, white flour, brown sugar, canned delicacies—the sort of luxuries that an over-reached group of whites might run out of first if an expected supply wagon were long in coming. The soldiers said nothing about helping with the wood supply, and no one asked them. Their watchful, nervous actions made it abundantly clear that they regarded the mission as hostile territory and were anxious to leave.

Gloriana's uncle saw the crushed expression on Gloriana's face and reached out a comforting hand to pat her drooping shoulder. "At least they brought something, my dear. That is considerably more than I expected. It seems you have made a rather profound impression on the young man." He pointed to the heavy envelope she was holding in her hand.

"But, Uncle, I don't understand. I prayed so hard and believed so strongly that help was coming," Gloriana brushed aside his reference to Lieutenant Tilton's letter; her voice was sharply edged with complaint, and from inside she sent a few reproachful why's heavenward.

Dr. Windemere smiled sadly, thought a moment, and then said quietly, "Gloriana, sometimes we have to stop and ask ourselves who we are believing in, ourselves and the people around us or God. If our faith is truly in Him, we will let God work out the way He answers our prayers and even leave it to Him whether the answer be yes or no."

"Miss Glory, your help came but too small," Oweena added somewhat smugly, Gloriana thought. "Now we see about Oweena's help."

CHAPTER 9

THE NEXT MORNING ACTUALLY DAWNED—for the first time in days. A thin ribbon of liquid yellow sunshine peered beneath the storm clouds in the east. By chapel time the ribbon had widened to a broad band of blue sky, and Dr. Windemere offered a prayer of thanks, both for the army's help (it is not our place to criticize anything the Lord sends, he told them) and for the promise of better weather. By noon the sky was clear with only a few clouds resting heavily on the mountains to remind the missionaries of their ordeal.

As if in response to the brightening skies, the sick showed signs of improvement, and for the first time since the start of the epidemic, fewer new cases were diagnosed than on the day before.

"This could be the break we have been praying for, or it could be just the eye of the storm," Dr. Windemere observed cautiously, but he went about sloshing through the great lakes of mud in the mission yard with renewed energy and even a song, off-key but cheerful all the same, on his lips.

Given a morning to herself, Gloriana decided to

wash her hair. She had avoided the task for several days because of the difficulty of drying it and because of a little soreness about her throat and chest. Now it was a relief to unbraid the thick coils of hair and to feel the warm, soapy water touch her scalp.

"When this epidemic is over, I am going to sleep for a week," she promised herself. Looking in her mirror, Gloriana was surprised to see the dark circles under her eyes, but the faint red flush beginning at the roots of her hair drew her incredulous gaze. 'No, it couldn't be!" she told herself, but she tore open the front of her dressing gown all the same. Tiny pink dots were already raised and, she realized suddenly, itching on her pale white skin. Still hoping to be wrong, she went back to the mirror and, opening her mouth, tried to peer inside. The light in the room with the wooden shutters half closed was dim, but she thought she could see the telltale Koplik's spots inside.

How long had it been since she had had measles? Ten years? Certainly it was possible to contract the disease more than once, but why now, and why here? She had worked with measles epidemics many times at home in Philadelphia and never had shown the slightest sign of infection.

Lord, I don't have time for this. You can't let it happen!

Opening the shutters to catch the sun, she began to dry her long hair. She noticed with some exasperation that the long strands were curling into tight little corkscrews in the still-damp air. The mass of dark hair fluffing out around her pale face brought back memories of Applegate Landing, and she found herself thinking about Graham Norton.

There had been little time for daydreaming during the past few weeks, but if there had been, she probably would have refused to think about the Westerner all the same. But now—perhaps it was the weakness brought on by her impending bout with this absurd children's disease—in any case, she could not seem to keep her mind from conjuring up pictures of Norton in a hundred different attitudes and actions— Norton driving a wagon with his hat tipped back and his red hair bobbing across his forehead like a flame; Norton loading freight or chopping wood, the thick corded muscles bulging and rippling beneath his shirt; and Norton holding her hand on the way to Blessing Waters, a tender excitement in his eyes and an almost shy grin on his lips.

"Am I falling in love with that wild, Western man?" she asked herself finally. The quick denial was not altogether convincing, even to Gloriana.

A dreamy half hour had passed when Gloriana was pulled out of her reverie by a commotion in the mission yard below. What she saw made her heart stop. And forgetting about the measles and the danger of infecting anyone, she pulled on a dark, open-necked dress without noticing how it accented her pallor and exposed the hectic flush of the rash on her neck and chest.

Below in the mission yard, Dr. Ralph Windemere was facing a band of three dozen Indians—all young warriors mounted on sturdy-looking mustangs and carrying full quivers of arrows with the bows draped across their backs. A sense of power and savagery surrounded the party like a tangible atmosphere, and Gloriana wondered if at last she were seeing the heartless war party that had committed so many atrocities.

The leader of the band was a chief; his authority was evidenced in his face rather than in any ostentatious ornaments. He sat as tall and straight on his prancing mustang as any of the younger men; only the iron-gray color of his hair and a heavily lined face betrayed his age.

Ralph Windemere held out his hands in the traditional gesture of welcome. For an instant there was no response; then a warrior who rode beside the chief dismounted and came toward the gathered missionaries.

"Keintepoos!" Gloriana heard a little gasp and turned to see that Oweena had joined her. The girl's glowing face told her story, and from the quick look thrown in their direction by the young giant, it seemed that he had not missed Oweena's presence.

Well over six feet tall, the warrior was strikingly handsome, with an air of command not unlike the leader's. His face was a smooth, sculpted mask except for the large dark eyes that seemed to see everything. Long raven hair had been tied with rawhide at the back of his neck, and the buckskin of his shirt stretched tightly across massive shoulders.

"So this is the reason Oweena has left her home," Gloriana thought, and for a moment she felt a little shiver of fear that somehow this lovely girl might have betrayed them. *But for what purpose? There is nothing to be gained by killing us or destroying the mission. No, Oweena is here because she loves this young warrior and he, whatever his feelings, has not yet asked her to be his bride.*

Gloriana remembered the hint of some secret sorrow that she had sensed in the girl. Reaching out to Oweena, Gloriana gave her arm an encouraging pat. The girl was shivering with excitement.

"I am Keintepoos, Chief of the Warricka. I speak for Chief John and the Federation of the Southern Tribes." The warrior's speech was clipped and commanding; his accent was foreign to Gloriana's ears, but the phrases were correct, suggesting a mission-school education. *Surely*, she thought, *if he has gone among us, he understands us, knows that we mean his people no harm.* Yet there was something ominous about the phrase "Federation of Southern Tribes," calling up images of natives united in uprisings, banded together against some common enemy.

77

If her uncle and Dr. Midfield shared her anxiety, they gave no indication. Their faces remained as courteously impassive as those of the chiefs. In fact, the two doctors, both small and fragile beside the magnificient physiques of the natives, seemed incongruously to exude an almost supernatural courage, and Gloriana was reminded of "Daniel in the Lions' Den," the first sermon she had heard Dr. Midfield preach.

Her uncle answered the chief gravely, speaking the formula phrases of welcome she recognized as, "We are honored by your visit. How may we help our brothers?" He spoke in Klamath, and the face of the old chief registered his pleasure at the courtesy.

"We hear of sickness," Chief Keintepoos continued. Then he added with a note of challenge that made Gloriana gasp, "We hear it kills many of our people. We hear it is red sickness made for red man by our white brothers."

Oweena let out a little cry, but the warrior did not glance in her direction.

"Our brothers" was all Gloriana could make out of her uncle's reply, but she supposed he was trying to explain that among whites measles is a children's disease. She supposed that it must seem strange to these people that in all of the weeks of the epidemic, none of the staff had become ill. Possibly they even imagined the staff were somehow responsible for the deaths; as soon as the missionaries diagnosed patients as having the disease, the patients would immediately become sicker. Even Oweena, who understood much of what was happening, had once expressed amazement at Gloriana's amazing ability to "predict" who would become ill.

Gloriana remembered too the persistent arguments of the Cayuse chiefs accused of the Whitman massacre a few years before. They had not denied the murders but had explained over and over again to the

78

tribunal that Cayuse law called for the killing of bad medicine men. Dr. Whitman had cured the white settlers but not the natives; therefore, he was a bad medicine man and had to be killed. The argument had seemed ridiculous at the time, and even later when Graham Norton had mentioned the chief's charges, Gloriana had found them so absurd that she imagined the man was purposely trying to provoke her. But now after living through the horrors of an epidemic with the Indians, feeling as they did the injustice of the disease that caused so much suffering among their ranks, she could understand the young chief's question and even sympathize with it.

Thank You, Lord, for having a right time for everything—even for catching measles, Gloriana breathed a prayer, and, adding a postscript to send her a quick dose of courage, she pulled away from Oweena's hand, which was clutching hers, and spoke softly in her uncle's ear.

A broad smile crossed the old man's face. "My dear, you are indeed manna from heaven—a fresh blessing with each day's new needs." He had to do no more than glance at the blotches clearly visible on her light skin to confirm the diagnosis. Then, putting his arm around her shoulders, he drew her toward the waiting Chief Keintepoos and began to explain her condition in a detached tone that she recognized as his best clinical manner, though she did not understand the words.

Gloriana's ready blush stained her neck and cheeks, accenting the rash further, as the warrior stepped forward to observe the symptoms her uncle was pointing out one by one. Keintepoos was apparently familiar with the signs, perhaps having suffered from the disease at sometime himself, for he insisted upon seeing the Koplik's spots in her mouth. But she began to suspect his motives when, after a lengthy examination of her tongue, she met his dark eyes for a moment and recognized the amusement lurking there.

79

Convinced, Keintepoos turned to speak to the waiting Chief John and his warriors. At last Gloriana breathed a sigh of relief; then she felt the pressure of her uncle's hand encouragingly on her shoulder, and she realized that instead of simply reporting her condition, the young chief had invited members of his band to examine her themselves.

For fully twenty minutes the imposing warriors pressed around Gloriana, eager, it seemed, to witness this phenomenon of a white woman with the red sickness. Remembering how amusing her young patients had found her, Gloriana strongly suspected that the warriors were also thoroughly enjoying her embarrassment. When they had finished their inspection, some of the Indians who had already been at the mission crowded forward for a look. All seemed especially interested in the Koplik's spots in her mouth, and again and again Gloriana stuck out her tongue and waited while the tiny red dots were pointed to and exclaimed over.

Even Oweena had to look, and her comment made Gloriana wonder once again how the beautiful girl viewed sickness and the role of the medical staff in treating it. "Miss Glory, why did you let this happen?" She also continued to see God as directly involved in the dispensing of illnesses. "Maybe Lord God is angry with you. Miss Glory must repent." The concern in the girl's face was so genuine that Gloriana felt touched in spite of the implications of her words. When the usually undemonstrative Oweena gave her a quick hug, Gloriana felt as though she truly belonged at Klamath Mission.

She longed to sit down. Her knees had begun to shake, and her stomach was beginning to roll ominously. Still the people came as though none was willing to be left out or to miss the chance of examining the mission nurse. In fact, a few, in imitation of Dr. Windemere's notorious poking finger, even gave her a few jabs and asked tentatively, "Hurt?"

The two chiefs had remained standing nearby throughout the ordeal, though after their first inspection, they did not seem to be watching her. Finally, when the last Indian had stepped off the porch, Chief John turned to Keintepoos with a rush of what sounded like orders in the Indian tongue.

Keintepoos stepped toward them then. He spoke to Gloriana's uncle, this time in Klamath, but she had the uncomfortable feeling that the warrior's eyes strayed laughingly to her face.

Dr. Windemere looked startled for a moment; then he turned to Gloriana and explained carefully, "My dear, it seems Chief John is very impressed with you. He feels you would be the mother of many brave warriors. Therefore, he would like you to become his fourth wife, provided of course you survive the red sickness. He is offering fifty horses for you —an impressive bride gift."

Gloriana had no idea what kind of reply was expected, but she had no need to make any. With an astonished glance at the two chiefs—both looking at her in a kind and almost gentle way—Gloriana, for perhaps the first time in her life, fainted.

She learned later about the remaining events of the day and felt she had learned more than one lesson in trusting God. With the good faith of the missionaries established, the chiefs had announced their intention to help. Orders had been given, and a long string of ponies had come into the mission yard—some laden with the carcasses of deer and elk, some carrying ears of unshucked corn in huge baskets balanced on each side of the animals like oversized saddlebags.

"I think they always intended to help us," her uncle told her late that afternoon. "They just had to test us a bit first." Through the closed shutters of her room, Gloriana could hear the steady ring of an ax,

81

witness to the warriors' helping with more than the food. The appetizing aromas of roasting venison and baking cornbread found their way from the cooking fires.

"I overheard some of the braves talking," her uncle continued with a chuckle. "They were saying how happy they would be to eat Indian food again; they do not seem to have enjoyed our oatmeal and chicken soups very much." He did not comment on God's wisdom in choosing His own deliverers for the mission, but Gloriana was sure her uncle felt it as much as she did.

Klamath Mission   October, 1851

I am in quarantine. Uncle Ralph feels that if I, with all my years of exposure, can contract measles again, the disease must have mutated, creating a new strain that could easily infect the entire mission staff.

Somehow I doubt there is much danger. The sickness has served its purpose. We have food and fuel again for the winter. Dr. Midfield is no longer blistering his hands trying to add to the wood stacks, and poor Catherine, who is having a harder pregnancy than she would admit, can take to her bed. The Klamath women, encouraged by the chiefs, have taken over supplying meals for the patients. Their corn mush—almost a corn chowder—is more appetizing than our hospital oatmeal, and the soups they prepare are flavored with some delicious herbs. I suspect the cooks are adding healing potions of their own to the recipes.

I have not talked with my good friend Oweena, yet I hear much that disturbs me. Uncle Ralph reports that his housekeeper Tildy complains constantly of Oweena's being absent late into the night. The girls who work at the mission live with Tildy in their own cabin, and Tildy sees herself as their substitute mother. I suppose they find her harsh and restrictive, yet she wishes only the best for them.

Oweena is so passionate and single-hearted; I fear for her if this young chief disappoints her or is killed or injured. I still cannot dismiss the suspicion that these warriors are somehow connected with the renegades who pursued our freight train. It does not seem possible that these fierce-looking braves have banded together for no other purpose than hunting or rescuing beleaguered Christian missionaries.

Still I'm sure I have never seen Chief Keintepoos or Chief John before, and there is something different about their native dress. Their hunting shirts are soft deerskin, stitched together with braided strips of hide, but I seem to remember the Indians who attacked us wore white tunics heavily embroidered across the chest and bound at the hips with sashes of brightly colored fringed material in red, purple, and green.

To try to focus the images in her mind, Gloriana began to sketch. She tried picturing Chief Keintepoos and his men, as she had seen the renegades—over Graham Norton's muscled shoulder, spears in their hands. As she sketched, the memories came more clearly. She remembered broad bands of red warpaint on cheeks and foreheads, bright pieces of cloth tied like sashes at the sides of their heads, long flowing hair that hung past their shoulders in ragged elf locks.

The more she sketched, the less any of the renegades looked like the friendly chiefs and their men. *The renegades are picturesque and oddly barbaric looking like I always imagined Indians to be* , she thought. *Keintepoos and his warriors are less exotic, but more manly.*

She put down her pencil for a moment and tried to go back in her mind to the wagon camp beside the stream to recapture every detail of the renegades' appearance. She could not escape the feeling that there was something she was missing, and it suddenly occurred to her that she would like to discuss the matter with Graham Norton. He knew these people; he would be able to figure out the reason for this faint suspicion hovering at the back of her mind like a cloud, that all was not as it seemed. For Oweena's sake as well as that of all the settlers, she had to find out whether Chief Keintepoos was a brutal murderer.

But when Gloriana picked up her pencil again a few minutes later, it was not the strong, high cheekbones of Keintepoos or the wildly glaring expressions of the renegades that her pencil drew but the square firm jaw and arrogantly handsome face of Graham Norton.

CHAPTER 10

TWO WEEKS HAD PASSED before Gloriana was permitted to leave her room; another week before she could again take an active part in mission life. In the meantime the number of new cases of measles had diminished daily until Dr. Windemere declared the epidemic was over. Gradually the encampment, which had grown almost to a small city, was dispersing back into the hills and grasslands. Only a few convalescents remained, and they occupied themselves with repairing tents and making arrows in preparation for their journey to sheltered winter camps.

The weather continued fair, the puddles dried, and a luxurious Indian summer settled over the wilderness. It was weather to dream rather than to work in and, finding her dreams returning uncomfortably often to Applegate Landing and an arrogant Westerner with eyes like blue flames, Gloriana recruited her energy and Oweena for a huckleberrying expedition.

Donning heavy, long-sleeved dresses to protect them against thorns in the berry patch, the girls set out for a promising tangle of vines that nearly filled a marshy hollow where a small stream emptied into the lake.

"I like your Keintepoos," Gloriana told Oweena as they picked their way at a leisurely pace among the rocks along the lakeshore.

"He's not mine," the girl protested quickly.

"But it's easy to see he's in love with you. His eyes when they follow you fairly smolder, and I know you care about him."

Oweena said nothing but picked up a rock and sent it skipping out into the lake. The action drew a protest and a shake of a fist from a small Klamath boy. Fishing from the edge of the lake with his willow pole, he had been sitting so still that neither girl had noticed him. Now he moved out on a rock to recast his line into the deep water below, as if Oweena had permanently disturbed the fishing at his earlier spot.

"Oweena, I hope you don't think I am meddling, but I am concerned about your happiness. Do you—that is, do the two of you have plans to marry?" Gloriana knew she was touching on delicate ground, but she sensed a softening in her close-mouthed friend and pressed further. "Were you perhaps once very close? Did something come between you?"

Giant tears squeezed from beneath lowered lashes before Oweena brushed them away with an angry hand.

"Keintepoos is too busy to marry. He follows warpath with Chief John, forgets Oweena."

"Who are they fighting?"

The girl did not reply, but after a moment she said, "Miss Glory, do you love the bluecoat who bring you here?"

"Why, no!" Gloriana was less surprised at the question than at the vehemence of her own answer.

"Oweena is very glad," was all her friend said, but it left Gloriana with the distinct impression that the bluecoats, as the Indians called the cavalry, were somewhere on that path of war Keintepoos and his braves had taken. Whether settlers and wagon trains were also on it, she would have to wait for another time to find out.

The afternoon passed quickly. All along the lakeshore the huckleberries grew in thick patches. The heavy rains, followed by warm sun, had made the berries grow fat and juicy, and the lush stocks, weighted down with fruit, trailed in the water. The girls filled their pails in spite of the inroads each made on the stores—smudging their lips and making purple rings around their mouths. Then Gloriana took off the bleached flour-sack towel she had wrapped around her waist for an apron, and they began to fill that.

"Tildy has to be impressed with this," Gloriana told the laughing Oweena, "Maybe she'll make us a huckleberry pie." And they took off their shoes to wade into the marshy water after clusters of berries that looked as large as their little fingers. They quickly stripped the fruit from the thorny bushes; ripe and heavy, it seemed to fall into their hands with no more than a touch. They had tucked their long skirts up between their legs and waded in deeper when they heard a sudden splash and a little yelp which was cut off abruptly by a gurgling sound.

A hundred feet behind them, the lake was churning frantically beneath a rocky overhang. In an instant Gloriana knew what had happened. The Indian boy, who had been fishing from the edge, had leaned over too far and fallen in. The dark blue color of the water below attested to the depth of the fishing hole, a sharp contrast to the surrounding blue-green lake. She watched for a second, expecting to see his head break the surface, for even the smallest Klamath boys were adept swimmers. When it did not, she realized he must have struck his head going down or perhaps become entangled in the roots of a nearby willow.

"Oweena, we've got to do something. Find a long

stick. Hurry!" Gloriana shouted. Splashing out of the berry patch, Gloriana was already running toward the rolling water. She tried not to take her eye off the exact spot where the boy had gone in.

"Dear God, help me get there in time!" Knowing that they would only hamper her movements and drag her down in the water, she pulled off her heavy dress and petticoat. She was glad she had already removed her shoes; their awkward buttons would have delayed her by minutes.

She had taken swimming lessons when she was a young girl. Her father had insisted, saying one never knew when an emergency might occur, but she had been an awkward pupil and had not practiced in years. "God, make me remember how," she had just time to breathe before she was at the lake's edge and plunging in.

The cold of the water hit her with a shock. In the shallow marshes where the berries grew, the autumn sun had been strong enough to penetrate and warm the waters; but in the deeper parts of the lake, the chill was more in keeping with the time of the year.

Her arm stroked the water awkwardly at first, then more smoothly as she found the lake waters buoying her up, helping her over the surface. It was only a few yards to the pool where the child had disappeared. Taking a big breath, she dove, kicking to get beneath the surface. The pool was in a shadow and so dark she could see nothing. She felt something slick and cold move against her arm and jerked away before she realized it must have been a fish.

Gloriana's lungs felt as though they would burst, and moving her arms and legs was becoming more and more difficult as the cold numbed them. She knew she would have to go up for air soon. Then her groping hand found a round head, and her arms circled a small limp body.

The few feet to the surface seemed like a hundred.

The boy was a dead weight in her arms, lighter in the water than out, she knew, but still a burden she was barely able to propel upward. Breaking through into the air, she took a deep breath, but the strength she hoped for did not flow into her body. A terrible weakness had invaded her limbs. For an instant she thought the child would slip from her grasp; then she remembered how to float and, turning on her back, held on desperately to the limp form while she fought for her breath.

Somewhere at the edge of consciousness Gloriana thought she heard a sound like hoofs pounding on the grassy lakeshore. She remembered Oweena and hoped the girl had found a long stick, for she knew she would not be able to climb the slight incline of the shore without something to hold onto.

"The Lord is the strength of my life," the words came back to her. And holding the child securely in one arm, she turned and began to crawl slowly, pushing with her legs and pulling with her one free arm toward the shore.

She was in a daze as she approached the lake side. She reached down and felt her feet touch the bottom, but she seemed powerless to climb the last few feet out of the water.

"Oweena," she almost whispered her friend's name and began looking around frantically for something to grasp.

Suddenly she was aware of someone running toward her, calling her name. The water around her rose and buffeted against her as someone leaped splashing and stumbling to her side. Then strong arms closed around her, lifting Gloriana and her burden.

On the shore a crying Oweena was reaching for them; the stick she had had no chance to use lay discarded nearby. She took the boy hastily from Gloriana and laid him on the grass.

Gloriana heard a sharp intake of breath and opened

her eyes to discover herself held tightly against a broad chest, and, lifting her gaze further, looked straight into the intent blue eyes of Graham Norton. Immediately she realized that his hands were grasping her bare legs and arm. The thin material of her wet chemise clung to her form, outlining and emphasizing every detail.

At any other time the modest Gloriana would have blushed furiously to be discovered in such a predicament, but now she had no time for embarrassment. Breathlessly she told Norton to put her down; then she rushed to the still, limp form of the child.

He had swallowed seemingly gallons of lake water. She pumped furiously, trying to get it all out of him, then showed Norton how and he pumped some more. Then pushing on his lungs in a rhythmic motion, she tried to revive the child, to coax his lungs to take a breath and his heart to start pumping again. For ten minutes she worked, the weakness of a moment before seemingly forgotten.

Oweena was sobbing softly and a grim Graham Norton was getting up the courage to persuade her to stop when the child coughed suddenly and began to take in great raspy breaths.

"We've got to get him back to Uncle and the hospital," Gloriana told a jubilant Norton. "Is your horse nearby? Can you take him?"

"He is, but in case you haven't noticed, it's nearly dark, and you're more than three miles from the mission. This is no place for women alone at night."

"But the child must have a doctor immediately!" she told him, exasperated. How could she have forgotten what an unyielding man Graham Norton was?

However, Norton had an alternative in mind. Turning to Oweena, he asked her quietly, "Can you ride bareback?"

She nodded briefly.

Then he was on his feet, stripping the saddle and blanket from his horse and mounting Oweena on the animal's back with the child cradled carefully in front of her.

"Now ride!" he told her and pointed the horse in the direction of the mission. Oweena needed no further instruction. She grasped the reins expertly in one hand while holding the Indian boy tightly against her with the other and with a quick jab of her heels propelled the swift horse into the long swinging stride of his running gait.

"Smart girl," Graham told Gloriana as they watched the pair quickly spring out of sight. "She'll keep him at a run and avoid jarring the boy with a gallop, and with her light weight they could make it all the way to the mission before he breaks gait.'

"Why did you take off the saddle?" Gloriana asked curiously. She was shivering now and feeling at last the embarrassment of her condition, but she was determined to keep up a polite conversation.

"So you could have this," he told her and, picking up the saddle blanket, shook it out and quickly wrapped it around her. The wool had a strong horsy smell and it made her itch, but the warmth from the big animal's body still clung to the blanket and felt delightful against Gloriana's icy skin.

Norton seemed to avoid looking in her direction while he flung himself into gathering wood and making a fire. Finally, he went in search of her clothes. Fortunately, she had not thrown anything into the water, and he soon returned with petticoat and dress. She had to send him back again for her shoes and stockings. They had not fared as well and somehow had been knocked into the water during their berry-picking. He had set them carefully by the fire when Gloriana remembered the huckleberries and sent him to find both the pails and the apron filled with fruit.

"Now Tildy can make her pies," she told him appreciatively when those too had been retrieved.

Behind the mountains to the west the sun was setting. The orange-gold rays struck the lake, setting it ablaze with dancing lights. In the enchantment of the moment Gloriana discovered Graham had somehow found his way to her side. His fingers reached out to wander playfully through her curling tangles of hair, then turned her face gently toward him.

Gloriana supposed she should push him away, but her hands were busy clutching the blanket around her. She was fascinated at how soft Graham's usually hard mouth could become as his lips moved gently on hers. The feather-light kisses teased and excited, tempting her to press her own lips tightly against his. Whether she gave in to the temptation or not, Gloriana was in too much of a daze to be sure, but suddenly Graham drew back. His breath was ragged and his voice, husky.

"Glory, you are such an innocent!" he tried to laugh. "Don't you know how enticing you are, how tempting being with you like this is to a man?"

Gloriana looked at him, wide-eyed and uncomprehending. The blanket had slipped slightly around her shoulders, exposing her white skin to the rosy glow of the firelight. What was he saying? She tried to think. Did he mean he had kissed her because it was what any man would do? Did he mean he did not care about her as a person but had found the situation and her vulnerability irresistible?

She was not aware of the mirror which her expressive face made for those thoughts, nor of the valiant struggle of the man who held her to control his baser instincts and protect her innocence. She did recognize the note of passion in his groan and the urgency with which his arms tightened around her. She tried to pull away but was helpless against the iron muscles pressing her against him.

What might have happened neither would know. Through the darkness came the creaking sound of wagon wheels, and both realized that help was on its way from the mission.

"Here! Put these on quickly now," Graham handed Gloriana her clothes. He turned his back and seemed to be glowering into the darkness.

Gloriana had the rumpled garments securely in place by the time the wagon emerged from around a forested bend and pulled into the firelight. Dr. Windemere was sitting on the front seat with Gloriana's old friend Smitty. Her uncle was on the ground and taking her pulse with an experienced hand before Gloriana had a chance to say she was all right or to ask about the little boy. To her embarrassment, he insisted upon looking inside her throat, though he could see little in the firelight, and listening at her chest with the stethoscope that still hung conveniently about his neck. She thought she caught a glimpse of Graham Norton looking on and laughing but supposed she was wrong; his sudden, inexplicable anger could not have dissipated so quickly.

Finally her anxious uncle was reassured enough to answer her questions.

"The boy will be fine. Midfield was still watching him when I left, but his breathing is regular. You did a fine job, my dear. The child has you to thank for saving his life." He then turned toward Graham Norton. "And if what I gather from Oweena's nearly hysterical story is accurate, we have you to thank for saving both of them. How can we repay you?"

Norton apparently interpreted the question as a rhetorical one, for he did not answer, but the two men clasped hands in a firm gesture that showed clearer than words a mutual respect. However, a moment later as they turned away to climb into the wagon, Gloriana thought she heard a short laugh and the words, "I'll think of something."

The wagon was a two-seated buckboard, its back seat piled high with blankets—probably sent by the quick-thinking Tildy when she heard about Gloriana's swim in the lake. Graham helped Gloriana up, then climbed up beside her, while Dr. Windemere scrambled in beside Smitty who handled the team.

"Wrap her in those blankets, Graham, or Tildy will have my head," the doctor confirmed Gloriana's guess, then turned back to speak to Smitty.

There was a little smile on Graham Norton's face as he carefully followed orders, perhaps tucking a bit more here and reaching around her a bit more there than was strictly necessary for Gloriana's comfort.

"That's quite enough," she told him after a moment. "Any more, and I won't be able to breathe."

The trip back to the mission went much more slowly than the trip out, but in spite of Smitty's care the jarring of the wagon made every bone in Gloriana's body ache. Graham noticing her discomfort, put a protecting arm around her and told her quietly to lean against him.

"You probably have strained every muscle and maybe picked up some bruises," he told her and threatened to call on her uncle for support if she would not do as he said. Blushingly aware of the two men in the front of the wagon, Gloriana tried resting ever so slightly against the strong arm that encircled her. She was soon forced to admit that Graham took much of the shock of bumps and dips for her and gradually found herself nestling more snugly in his arm. Although her uncle glanced back at them from time to time, he gave no sign of noticing that his niece was in the embrace of a man. However, after a glance or two, he did seem to become excessively cheerful, even beginning to whistle the Doxology in his off-tune way and to a totally inappropriate, lilting rhythm.

It took more than half an hour to reach the mission. To Gloriana's surprise they found the cozy living room of the main cabin occupied not only by the mission staff and two or three of Norton's men but also by a family of settlers.

"They came up from San Francisco on the same packet you took," Graham explained hastily to Gloriana. She filled in the rest, imagining the trip overland through the redwoods and then a delightful stop at Applegate Landing.

Roger Welsh was the man's name and he proudly introduced his large family. There was his wife Eugenia, a pale, washed-out woman whose drooping shoulders and listless face showed the effects of too much work and too much childbearing. Five sons ranged in age from about twenty-six to three, and for a moment, Gloriana looked at the fairy-like daughter Bridgette. She felt a rush of intense pleasure as she realized how much the girl looked like her own sister Juliana.

"I am sure we will be great friends," she said impulsively, then immediately regretted the words as she realized the pale blue eyes in the china doll face were cold and calculating.

But it was too late to retract. Bridgette rose to offer her hand, all the while casting sly glances at Graham from under eyelashes that fluttered provocatively. "Thank you, Miss Windemere," she said in a voice that oozed with sweetness and trembled slightly, as though to show how timid and overwhelmed she actually was. "I can't tell you how much it will mean to me to have an older friend like you—someone I can rely on for advice and spiritual guidance."

Gloriana barely suppressed a little gasp, and behind her she thought she heard Graham Norton swallow a laugh.

CHAPTER 11

IN THE DAYS THAT FOLLOWED, the briefly placid mission became once again a hub of frenzied activity. Graham Norton's project for Dr. Windemere was a quadrangle of buildings including a large steeple-topped church to replace the original chapel. The men soon added an orphanage to their plans, for the epidemic had left the mission with nearly twenty homeless children to care for.

"We'll get the walls up and the roofs on before snow flies," Norton said confidently. "Then we can spend the winter putting in floors and finishing up the insides."

It seemed incredible that so much could be done in such a short time. But as the nearby forest rang with the sound of axes and the heavy mule teams churned up dust pulling the straight, sweet-smelling logs to the mission, it began to seem possible.

The site of the building activity was set back from the lake in a sheltered saddle of land. Framed by the log cabins was a beautiful artesian spring, bubbling up from deep inside the ground with such force that

Graham said it would neither freeze in the winter nor dry up in the summer. Giant willows bent possessively over the water; their great girth and luxuriously sweeping branches attested to both the faithfulness of the spring and the richness of the land.

Gloriana had little time to savor the enlargement of her community, for the hospital was busy once again. Colds and pneumonia, aggravated by the deceptive weather—mild during the day but dropping lower each night—afflicted the resident Klamaths, while three of the women who had had measles had given birth to babies with congestion already in their lungs.

Equally distressing were the attacks on miners and settlers by the renegade war party. One man, surprised panning gold only a few miles from the mission had been robbed, scalped, and left for dead. A family of Swedish dairy farmers—too unfamiliar with the language to do more than identify their attackers as Indians—had seen their home on the Lost River burned and looted as they brought their cows in for the evening milking. They had escaped, but others had not. Word came by travelers and scouts of burned cabins and missing wagon trains, and almost daily the wilderness hid more unmarked graves.

For Gloriana the attacks brought the added burden of doubt. She could not help wondering if their Indian friends were responsible for those atrocities. There had been no problem with the renegades during the measles epidemic, but now reports were increasing daily. Moreover, it seemed the war party had shifted its activities from the coast and Applegate Landing to the area immediately surrounding Klamath Lake. That this shift had almost coincided with the arrival of Chief John and Keintepoos deepened her suspicions, though she kept reminding herself of the different costumes of the renegades she had seen.

"But how do I know they don't dress differently when they're on the warpath?" Gloriana asked herself. She was on her knees scrubbing the floor of the small alcove of the hospital that served as a baby ward. Some of the Klamaths who resided at the mission would have helped her, she knew, but she also was well aware that they found her passion for soap and water astonishing, to say the least. Although they would use hot water and soap every crack and corner if she kept after them, the Klamaths found her demands unreasonable, and to avoid offending them by barking like a drill sergeant, Gloriana preferred to do the job herself.

Moreover, working physically would usually take her mind off her problems. Today, however, was an exception, and her mind chewed trouble like a dog a dry bone—distastefully but relentlessly.

"Need some help?"

She looked up in exasperation to see one of her major troubles, Graham Norton, grinning at her from the open doorway. He had what appeared to be a picnic basket over one arm and looked rather boyishly handsome with his head uncovered and his flame-red hair curling damply as though he had washed away the grime of his morning's toil by ducking his entire head and face in a bucket.

"You didn't come to lunch, so Tildy sent me with this," he said cheerfully, holding up the basket. He seemed oblivious to the indignity of her condition, but Gloriana was acutely aware of the wet strands of hair straying across her cheeks and forehead, her soapy arms with the sleeves rolled up above her elbow, and her wet and grimy uniform.

"I can't imagine what possessed her to send you," Gloriana faltered. Then realizing how ungracious she sounded, she added, "That is, Tildy should know how busy you are." She continued kneeling on the floor, not knowing which would be more awkward—remaining in that position or struggling to her feet.

Graham settled the matter by grasping her arm with

98

his free hand and pulling her up beside him. "I volunteered," he told her, still grinning, and before she knew what was happening, Gloriana found herself outside beneath a willow tree, ready for a picnic lunch.

Tildy's food was, as usual, delicious, but the quantity as well as the extra treats showed clearly that this lunch had been made as much for Graham, who was a great favorite with Dr. Windemere's housekeeper, as for Gloriana. There was chicken pie—a delicious filling of egg and chicken meat in a tart of flaky pie crust—thick wedges of goat cheese to be eaten with slices of freshly baked bread, a potato salad dressed with Tildy's special mayonnaise, and enormous slices of huckleberry pie for dessert.

"I can see you have gotten on Tildy's good side," Gloriana laughed as she surveyed the contents of the basket.

"Amazing woman, that Tildy," Graham admitted readily. "Good source of information, too. For instance, how else would I have found out about my archrival?"

Gloriana paled slightly, and he seemed to notice, for he added wryly, "I am talking about Chief John, of course."

"Of course," Gloriana repeated quickly, then went on to tell him about the momentous day when she had attracted the chief's attention. "I'll have you know the chief considered me such a prize that he offered Uncle fifty horses for me," she concluded.

"I'll give him a hundred," Graham shot back softly with another of the dangerous smiles that seemed to turn Gloriana's insides upside down, sending her heart up into her throat and making her breath come in little gasps.

The tension of the moment was relieved by their determined attack on Tildy's food. By the time most of it was gone, Gloriana's embarrassment had passed, and she was ready to talk to Graham about what had been bothering her all morning.

She told him about her own early suspicions and then her doubt that the renegades and the war party that had helped the mission could be the same. "Still Oweena admits that they are on the warpath," Gloriana finished, feeling at once relieved to have voiced her fears and disloyal for repeating her friend's words.

Graham seemed puzzled but skeptical. "I understand your wish for their innocence. I feel the same. Still, if we look at it from the Klamaths' point of view, they have every right to wage war on the people who have invaded their lands. Besides, if it is not Keintepoos and Chief John, who could it be? What other tribes are on the warpath?"

Gloriana had no answer for that, but she still did not feel satisfied, and some of her earlier exasperation with Graham Norton returned.

"I'll keep my eyes open," he said—rather offhandedly, Gloriana thought. "For now I had better get back to my crew, or they will think it's a holiday." He rose and, after stretching lazily, headed for the doctor's cabin with the remains of their picnic lunch. Just before the path ducked around the corner of the hospital, he turned and winked teasingly at Gloriana. "Remember to tell your uncle about my offer." He was gone before she could think of what he meant; then she remembered the hundred horses and blushed hotly.

"If Graham Norton thinks that will serve for a proposal, he is sadly mistaken," she said so loudly that she woke several patients inside the hospital from their afternoon naps. She ignored, for the moment, the fact that she had somehow made the tacit assumption that the man would propose and that he was, indeed, thinking of marriage.

She had found her way back to her cleaning and had

just fetched a fresh supply of hot water when the squeaking board just inside the entrance to her small ward signaled yet another visitor. Glancing over her shoulder, Gloriana was not surprised to see Bridgette Welsh. The Welshes had decided to make their winter home in one of the new cabins at the mission and then move on to their own land in the spring. In the meantime Bridgette had attached herself firmly to Gloriana, relying, as she said frequently, upon the "older woman's advice."

"What can I do for you, Bridgette? I'm busy getting ready for some new arrivals," was Gloriana's discouraging greeting. She feared she would have sunk to absolute rudeness before spring came.

"I'm sorry to be such a bother," the girl began hesitantly, taking a short step backward and faltering in the timid way men seemed to consider so endearing. Gloriana found it unbearably irritating.

"Did you want something?" she prodded, letting the impatience creep into her voice.

"Well, if it isn't too much trouble, I just wanted your advice. You seem to know Graham Norton so well—that is, you seem to be such good friends; I thought you would be able to tell me whether you thought this dress would be appropriate for a moonlight walk by the lake." She twirled around to give Gloriana the full effect of a tight-waisted gauze and lace creation in a shade of blue that enhanced the blond beauty's fragility and air of innocence.

"Don't you think you should ask the man to take you before you plan what to wear?" Gloriana's tone held only a little of the exasperation she felt with this simpering miss.

"Why, Miss Windemere, whatever must you think of me? A lady never asks a gentleman, and I hope I have not forgotten that. Mr. Norton has already requested my company, of course."

To the repeated inquiry about the obviously summer dress, Gloriana managed some comment about the evening chill along the lake. She did not miss the little gleam of triumph in Bridgette Welsh's eyes and for the thousandth time wished her own face were not quite so revealing of her thoughts.

She did not think for a minute that the girl's insinuations were true. Graham Norton had shown much more than a friendly interest in Gloriana herself. Hadn't she been certain just today that his intentions toward her were serious, that he was beginning to think about marriage? Still she remembered wondering that night by the lake whether Graham's ardor was the product of too much moonlight and a romantic campfire.

Moreover, men did seem enchanted with Bridgette Welsh. She had the qualities that Gloriana had always found most deficient in herself. Where Gloriana was strong and self-reliant, Bridgette was like the society dolls back home in Philadelphia, waiting to lean on a man's strong arm and cling helplessly while he faced life's trials alone. Gloriana tended to speak her mind and never worried about deferring to men's opinions; Bridgette seemed to have no thoughts in her own head and waited only to hear some man's ideas before adopting them for her own. And where Gloriana had her share of beauty in flawless skin, glorious hair, and a full womanly figure, she felt like a Juno—huge and awkward—beside petite, graceful Bridgette.

Even Uncle calls her a "delightful girl," Gloriana thought with just a trace of resentment at the blindness of men.

Norton usually took his evening meal with the Windemeres, and tonight was no exception. They sat at a round, carved dining table which, unlike most of their furniture, had been carefully finished. A white tablecloth, silver, and china made the meal seem almost like dining back home, and Gloriana continu-

ally appreciated this ritual of civilization that reminded her each evening of their roots and their ambitions
for the wilderness.

Dr. Windemere, who preferred to give his thanks
for a meal after, rather than before, it had been eaten,
began on his roast venison with a gusto that promised
to add more pounds to his already ample girth.

"My Klamath weatherman tells me that it will snow
soon," the doctor told Graham. "I have never known
him to fail. Do you think the cabins will be roofed in
time?"

The progress on the new buildings had been little
short of miraculous. In just a matter of days walls had
risen and stone fireplaces had been built and tested.
Loads of an attractive red clay had been hauled in
which would later on make a kind of plaster for the
inside walls, and the men had split stacks of heavy
shake shingles that would be laid in overlapping rows
for a watertight roof.

"We need two more days of clear weather, so
remember that in your prayers," Graham answered
with a humorous glance in Gloriana's direction.

"I will do so," Dr. Windemere returned seriously,
before changing the subject to a German philosopher
named Kant, whose works he and Norton had been
reading.

At first Gloriana had been startled to hear that
Graham Norton, the gun-packing Westerner, was
interested in philosophy, but the man, as she was
learning, was full of surprises. Moreover, she was
beginning to suspect that philosophy was a way to
escape something he could not bring himself to face in
his own spirit.

Tonight, as on many other nights, the subject was
goodness and moral behavior. Graham advocated a
universal moral law which he said was a law of nature.

"The only good possible in this life," he was
saying, "is a good will. Otherwise, what is my good

may not be your good. What's good for the white man is rarely good for the Indians. We bring them civilization, which for us is good but for them means loss of dignity, sickness, and degradation."

"There is a higher good," Dr. Windemere responded, "and that goodness is God Himself. His good will extends beyond this short life into the next one and even goes so far as to blend the up-and-down patterns of individual existence to 'work together for our good'."

Usually Gloriana joined in their spirited discussions, but tonight she only listened. She had no doubt that Graham Norton was a good man according to his own standards. She knew that he would not intentionally do anything to hurt anyone. Yet she knew just as surely that his own moral code allowed him much more latitude than her Christian principles allowed her. If he felt that no one would be hurt by his actions, he would have no remorse, he said, about violating any of Christianity's laws. Did that include the laws of marriage, the special bonds and sacraments that Christ had established for the family and for the love of men and women? Could a woman ever fully trust a man who did not share her beliefs and values?

"Gloriana, my dear, I have spoken twice," Dr. Windemere broke through her musings to request a fresh cup of coffee and more of Tildy's buttery popovers.

Gloriana felt Graham's eyes follow her curiously as she hurried from the room.

You might as well come right out and tell him something's bothering you, Gloriana scolded herself angrily.

After dinner the men enjoyed a quiet pipe by the fireplace—a luxury which Graham's thoughtfulness in bringing an ample supply of tobacco had enabled the doctor to enjoy once again.

He is a good man—in many ways, Gloriana

reminded herself; then the vague suspicion planted in her mind by Bridgette's visit to the hospital returned, and she remembered for the first time in days that Graham Norton would not be good for her unless he shared her faith. Making an excuse about being tired, Gloriana tried to escape to her room, only to have Graham follow her.

"We'll find out the truth soon enough, Glory," he told her softly, and glancing over his shoulder to see if her uncle were watching, he touched her gently and looked longingly at her lips.

He thinks I'm really worried about the renegades, Gloriana thought. She knew she should move but it seemed she was rooted in place, held by the masculine appeal and fascination of this complex man.

"Graham, how about a game of chess?" her uncle's call broke the spell, and Gloriana retreated thankfully to her room where she alternately wrote in her journal and dreamed away the next hour.

Klamath Mission   November 7, 1851

Life at the mission has grown more complicated with the new arrivals. Graham Norton and his men follow their own schedule of dawn-to-dusk work. Rarely is there a moment when the air is not filled with the sounds of axes chopping or men shouting.

They treat the religious life of the mission with respect, and I suspect that several of the younger men remember Christian homes, but they do not join us. Once Smitty stepped into chapel for a few minutes, but he left after the song service was over.

The Welshes are of another faith, and so they do not attend our services either. I know our Indian flock wonders why the white people do not worship together. I do not know how to tell them that all our people do not follow the Jesus way; I don't think they would understand that it is possible for people to know about Christ, yet not follow Him—or follow Him in such different ways that we must have many different churches to express our belief in Him.

105

Sometimes I find myself looking back almost longingly to the days of the epidemic when all at the mission seemed united in a common cause. I cannot help thinking how much easier the Klamaths are to reach than are our own people. With them there are no elaborate philosophical or doctrinal differences to overcome; they simply hear and believe.

Uncle told me that when the fur traders first came to this country, they brought Bibles for use at funerals and weddings. They told the Indians only that it was the White Man's Book of Heaven and that teachers would come later to tell them the way. Yet no teachers came, and finally four Nez Perce chiefs traveled east to St. Louis to ask the missionaries to come. Two of the chiefs died on the way. The remaining two wrung the hearts of the Christians when they asked what had happened to the teachers. "My people," one of the chiefs said, "will die in darkness and they will go a long path to other hunting grounds. No white man will go with them and no white man's Book will make the way plain."

I think of those words whenever the hardships make me question our being here and whenever I wonder whether God is blessing our efforts. But always the valiant appeal of those chiefs will remind me of how these people hunger for God and how we, who have been blessed with so much knowledge, take Him for granted.

Hardly an hour had passed before Gloriana heard voices below signaling the end of the chess game. At Graham Norton's good-night call, almost involuntarily, she turned down her lamp and, going to the window, opened the shutters slightly so that she could watch the man cross the compound.

A half moon lit the scene with a pale gold light. On the chill air came the sound of Graham's whistling—more tuneful than her uncle's. In the distance a cabin door opened, and Gloriana could hear the faint, high-pitched sound of a woman's laughter.

He walked with a leisurely step, stopping to look toward the lake and once appearing to glance toward her window. His own quarters were in one of the far north cabins, and he seemed to be moving steadily toward it—past the chapel, past the schoolhouse, across the quadrangle. She had nearly closed her shutters when the tall form took a sharp right, and Gloriana realized that he was entering the Welsh cabin. She did not wait to see whether he emerged again with the dainty Bridgette on his arm but fastened her shutters securely and went to bed with a little coldness about her heart which even nighttime prayers could not entirely dispel.

CHAPTER 12

DR. WINDEMERE'S "WEATHERMAN" proved once again his accuracy as the mission woke the next morning to a light dusting of snow. Overnight the temperature had dropped thirty degrees, and the golden sky of Indian summer had changed to the pale gray of winter.

Cold inside as well as out, Gloriana hurried through her day at the hospital, wishing for something to happen that would take her mind off Graham Norton.

"It's none of my business what he does," she reminded herself several times. Perhaps unnecessarily she added, "I am not in the least bit jealous of that little minx."

But she still felt curiously depressed, and she tried not to notice the looks of concern that Oweena sent cautiously in her direction or mind Dr. Windemere's heavy-handed teasing about her "red-haired beau."

The diversion she had hoped for came late that afternoon from a totally unexpected direction. Gloriana had finished her work and drifted to the window of the tiny children's ward to watch the storm. Snow had been falling for the past hour, but it seemed to come from high in the sky in great feathery flakes that floated leisurely to the ground, decorating the landscape without obscuring their view.

From her special vantage point Gloriana was the first to see them coming—a long straggling line of blue-coated soldiers. The ragged line and drooping riders told her before she could see the makeshift bandages that something was wrong.

Dr. Windemere and Dr. Midfield were both in the hospital, and, alerted by Gloriana's warning, they hurried to check their medical supplies. Gloriana and Oweena began to make up beds for the casualties. Oweena was oddly silent, but when Gloriana tried to draw her out, she responded readily enough.

She's worried about Keintepoos and the Indian braves, Gloriana thought, realizing that she shared that worry. Somehow the brave Indian men who had helped the mission seemed closer to her now than the soldiers who represented the faraway government of her country.

It took nearly half an hour for all the soldiers to ride into the mission. About half were wounded, five or six seriously, but all suffered from loss of blood and exposure. Lieutenant John Tilton was last. A dark stain marked his right trouser leg just above the knee, and he was reeling in the saddle, but he held his rifle ready across the saddle horn and his head turned continuously to check for pursuers.

"The renegades caught us at night," he told them as the mission staff eased the officer from his horse. "Burned the stockade. Wiped out Linkville. It was Keintepoos and Chief John." Then he slipped into unconsciousness.

Treatment for the men's wounds was complicated by the hours they had spent in the saddle. The attack had come, they said, before dawn, two days earlier. They had fought for twelve hours before abandoning the stockade and beginning a fighting retreat north. Blood had flowed and caked or frozen, making it necessary to soak their clothing before removing it. Boots had to be cut off swollen feet, for some had walked to save their horses for the fifty-mile flight. Already, open flesh showed the red edges and whitish pus that signaled infection.

Since the epidemic had left the mission low on cleansing agents, the doctors resorted to cauterizing wounds, and the sickening smell of burning flesh was added to the heavy hospital odors. At first Gloriana had been called on to hold the men through that agony, but her strength had proved unequal to the task, and some of the men in Graham Norton's crew had been applied to for help.

Graham himself had come with the first sign of trouble and had helped with the heavy work of lifting and undressing the men. He had looked sober while the soldiers told of the attack and cursed Keintepoos and his men, but he said nothing.

"What do you think of your Indian friends now?" Gloriana overheard Graham asking Dr. Windemere when their separate duties had brought them momentarily together. The doctor had said nothing but had shaken his head sadly, as though not understanding what was happening and not caring to speculate.

Oweena, who had been going about her work with an increasingly dark expression, also overheard. She turned to Gloriana and whispered angrily, "He did not do it. Keintepoos would not kill the people of Linkville."

Gloriana was more struck by what Oweena had not said than by what she had said, for Oweena did not deny that the warriors might have attacked the soldiers.

"Why is she so angry?" Lieutenant Tilton, whose bandages Gloriana had been checking, opened his eyes to ask.

"She's a good friend of Keintepoos," Gloriana spoke before she thought, then immediately regretted it. The cold speculative gleam in the officer's eye was unmistakable.

More than eight hours passed before all the wounded were treated, and the long watch for fever and complications began. In the mission kitchen the coffeepot once again bubbled day and night on the back of the black iron range, but now the dark brew was a mixture of grains with just a flavoring of their precious store of coffee. Graham and Gloriana sat on opposite sides of the rough, split-log table. Tildy had gone to take Gloriana's place beside the sick soldiers, and Dr. Windemere was resting on a cot in his hospital office. The stillness of the empty cabin was broken only by the ticking of a clock in a room somewhere behind them. Outside, the still-falling snow absorbed the night sounds of the mission, replacing them with an almost oppressive silence.

Gloriana had wriggled out of her shoes and wrapped her throbbing feet in her long skirt. Her back ached, and there was a dull, pulsing pain at her temples. Yet she was not too tired to feel a little glow of triumph as she remembered that Bridgette Welsh had been conspicuously absent all afternoon and evening. *That should show Graham how self-centered she is,* Gloriana thought, although she was honest enough to admit that he might consider Bridgette's helplessness attractively feminine. She glanced at him from beneath lowered lashes, wondering what he was thinking about. His big-boned hands held a brimming tin cup in front of him; his eyes seemed intent on the thin cloud of steam rising from the dark liquid; their expression was dark and brooding.

"I wish you hadn't told the lieutenant about Oweena and Keintepoos," Graham said finally, meeting her gaze seriously.

Gloriana flushed and looked down before she

111

admitted honestly. "So do I! The look on his face as soon as I said it made me want to kick myself." She hesitated a moment. "Graham, there's something I don't understand about this."

A little grin tugged at the edge of the man's mouth, puzzling her, until Gloriana realized that she had unconsciously used his first name. "The lieutenant said Keintepoos and Chief John attacked the fort, and even Oweena doesn't deny that they might have. Yet the lieutenant also calls them the renegades, as though they are the ones responsible for killing settlers and harming women and children, and I don't think that can be."

"Why can't it?" The lazy smile vanished, and Graham was all interest.

"Well, Oweena says Keintepoos would not kill settlers. She says he would not have massacred the people of Linkville."

"But couldn't she be mistaken? I gather she's in love with him."

Gloriana nodded briefly, acknowledging Graham's unspoken assumption that love could cloud a person's judgment. "Perhaps there is more than one band of renegades," she admitted, "but I am convinced that Keintepoos had nothing to do with taking our supplies when we were on the road to Applegate Landing." She told him about her sketches, and he asked to see her journal.

Soon they were occupied in studying her drawings. As Gloriana explained her suspicions and showed him the results of her attempts to remember, she was struck again by the difference between Keintepoos's warriors and the renegades who had shadowed the freight train.

"Oweena has told me that the warriors of each tribe have a characteristic costume, but the renegades don't dress like any of the Indians I have seen."

"Or like any of the tribes from around here,"

Graham added. "These shirts and the sashes look almost like the Navajo garb, but I have never heard of Navajos ranging this far north and west. There's some mystery here—something we're not seeing."

Gloriana looked up and found their faces just inches apart.

"I don't like your being involved in this," he told her, his voice softening suddenly, "but it seems you are whether I like it or not." The possessiveness in his manner sent a little thrill through Gloriana. "And I'm going to need your help to find out what's going on."

"What can I do?"

Graham looked for a moment as though he would put his arms around her but settled instead for taking her hand in both of his.

"Watch John Tilton!"

CHAPTER 13

THE ATMOSPHERE OF THE MISSION changed dramatically during the next few days, and with the snowfall—an accumulation of six inches on the ground and more choking the mountain passes—there seemed little likelihood of another change before spring. Instead of blending in a harmonious community, the different groups at the mission withdrew into themselves. The Indians became aloof and somber, while Graham Norton's work crew and the soldiers squared off warily, each watching the other with thinly veiled hostility.

The daily rituals of chapel and hospital rounds continued, but always in the background there were small groups of blue-uniformed men, watching and snickering about "Injuns that get religion" or glowering about Eastern busybodies' trying to "heal savages so they can kill more white men."

"The soldiers are destroying our work," Gloriana complained to Dr. Windemere. They were sitting beside a roaring fire in what Tildy liked to call the parlor. It was a rugged but comfortable room dominated by a massive stone fireplace that nearly covered one wall. Above the polished mantelpiece in the place of honor was an ornately carved peace pipe, a gift to Dr. Windemere from the Klamath chiefs when he had first sought to found a mission on the lake. The head of the pipe was carved from red pipestone, a rare substance in Oregon Territory and, therefore, probably passed from hand to hand over thousands of miles of trading; the smooth bowl ended in a rounded hatchet, symbol of the ill fortunes that would befall anyone who broke the sacred compact. With the pipe the chiefs had also presented the doctor with a sheepskin deed to three hundred acres of lakeshore land. Most importantly to Dr. Windemere, the pipe and the land had been clear gestures not only of friendship but also of welcome, and on that foundation he had built a work to last long after his Heavenly Father called him home.

His eyes were on the peace pipe as he tried to frame an answer for his niece. But even the memories of all that the Lord had done could not quite keep the discouragement from his voice. "Not destroying, my dear, but certainly setting us back."

They spoke in low tones, for both remembered that Lieutenant Tilton was lying in a small room at the back of the house. He had been moved just the day before when his bed in the hospital had been needed for an elderly Klamath who had succumbed to the twin winter maladies of pneumonia and frostbite. The lieutenant was no longer in danger, yet he was far from well enough to take up residence with his men. One of the half-finished log houses in the sheltered quadrangle served the soldiers as a barracks. The fireplaces were working overtime, but even the hottest fires could not keep the cold from the unfloored buildings.

"Can't we send them to Fort Winnemucca or even back to Applegate Landing?" Gloriana persisted, sure

115

there must be some way to rid the mission of the disruptive soldiers.

"If I remember right, it was only recently that you were hoping and praying they would come," her uncle chided Gloriana gently. "We just have to keep believing that God has some plan in all of this."

Gloriana was silenced but not altogether satisfied. She did not see how God's work could be advanced nor Himself glorified by the mission's spending an anxious winter waiting for a fight to break out between the soldiers and Norton's workers, or for someone to run off with an Indian girl and set the peaceful mission Klamaths on the warpath. Moreover, she did not like the idea of having the troublesome lieutenant living in her own home. She supposed she should be thankful to have him close by; after all, Graham Norton had asked her to keep an eye on John Tilton. Where could she better do that than in the Windemere cabin? Yet she had become conscious during his days in the hospital of a warmth in the man's eyes as they followed her, and she felt oddly uncomfortable.

"No, I fear this is a mountain we must climb rather than move," her uncle had gone on, "and only the Lord knows what we will find on the other side."

They sat in silence for a few moments, Gloriana idly filling in the details of a sketch that she had begun earlier in the day.

"Well, if we can't change the make-up of the community, let's change its attitude," she told her uncle finally and launched into a plan that had been stirring in her mind for days. It was nearly the end of November; only three days remained until the twenty-sixth, the day which President Washington had proclaimed a National Day of Thanksgiving in 1789. There had been some talk about making that day a national holiday, but the Windemeres had not waited for any official proclamation. In their home and church, they had regularly celebrated Thanksgiving for many years.

"What better way to bring all Americans together?" she persisted as Dr. Windemere shook his head doubtfully. "We'll recreate the first Thanksgiving feast when the Pilgrims and the Indians joined together in friendship as we at the Klamath Mission should be joined. And it will give you a chance to preach a true Thanksgiving message and remind all the people here of the real purpose of this community."

The good doctor wavered, but Gloriana's last point won him over. He had often said that the only way to end the fighting was to bring all Oregon peoples together in the worship of the one true God; then the senseless massacres would end, and this glorious golden West could become the paradise that Indians and settlers alike dreamed of.

"We'll do it!" he told her enthusiastically.

There was still Tildy to be won over. That conscientious housekeeper's first reaction was to throw up her hands and plop her stout form on the nearest kitchen chair. "Lands, child! Feed more than two hundred people at Thanksgiving dinner in just short of three days? It can't be done!"

Leaving her uncle to deal with his faithful Tildy, Gloriana donned her boots and hooded winter cloak to take the news of their plan to the Midfield cabin. Outside, the late afternoon glow in the west was dimming to twilight. Her eyes intent on stepping in other footprints in the snow, Gloriana did not see Graham until she nearly collided with him. Gloriana told him about the Thanksgiving feast, and she was annoyed when he continued to smile his amused, indulgent smile.

"I guess it takes a party to get a pretty female all worked up," he said finally.

"But it's not just a party. It's a celebration of thanks. Don't you see? We will get everyone to break

117

bread together, just like the Pilgrims and the Indians. Then perhaps we can be friends."

"It will take more than breaking bread to make some of the people here friends," Graham told her skeptically. But in spite of his skepticism, he soon found he had promised to have his men erect temporary tables in the partially completed chapel, and he had even offered to supply venison and pheasants for the feast. Moreover, he followed along through the twilight toward the Midfield cabin, Gloriana's mittened hand tucked in the crook of his arm while his face wore a bewildered grin.

"Gloriana, Mr. Norton!" Catherine Midfield welcomed them. The summer glow in the cold-nipped faces made her exchange a significant look with her husband as they ushered the beaming couple into their cozy sitting room. Flowered drapes hung at the windows, braided rugs covered the floors, and enough bric-a-brac to warm the heart of any New England matron covered the furniture. Gloriana had made her own contribution to the back-East atmosphere with a pair of Boston watercolors done from memory—one of the Old North Church from whose tower had come the signal for Paul Revere's immortal ride and one of a triple-masted sailing vessel riding majestically amid smaller craft in the bay.

The Midfields too had been regular observers of Thanksgiving and were excited by the idea of resuming the custom in the West.

"If only we had some cranberries!" Catherine exclaimed wistfully. She had borne frontier life cheerfully, but as the time for her baby's arrival drew nearer, the woman's homesickness had become more urgent, evoking the pity and the concern of her friends.

"He seems like a dedicated man, but I don't think they will stay out here for long," Graham commented when he and Gloriana were once more out in the snow.

"Catherine misses home and church socials, and she's worried about raising a child out here." Gloriana would have confided more, but at that moment a treacherous ice slick hidden by the snow pulled her feet from under her. Graham grabbed for her but too late and instead of keeping them both upright landed with Gloriana in a heap of snow.

Anxiously Graham pulled himself up and bent over the still prone girl. The laughing face calmed his fears, and Gloriana began to tell him of winter mornings spent tobogganing and ice skating in Philadelphia.

"I didn't know proper young ladies did those things!" Graham seemed both delighted and amazed as he helped her to her feet, taking full advantage of the opportunity to let his arms encircle her.

"But you see, I was never a very proper young lady."

He grinned and pulled her close. "I never did care much for those delicate, proper creatures."

"Really? I thought that every man adored the pale, fragile type." Gloriana cast a flirtatious look at him from beneath long sweeping eyelashes, but Graham would not rise to the bait.

"Glory, don't flirt with me unless you mean it," he told her with a grin and a little squeeze that suggested what might happen if she ignored his warning.

Although she had planned to go only to visit the Midfields, Gloriana decided now to go on to the Welsh cabin. The pioneer family had been settled in a building that would one day be the mission's administrative offices. Two stories high, it made a spacious winter home, although Gloriana privately wondered if the settlers properly appreciated her uncle's generosity in allowing them to occupy it.

Of all the inhabitants of the mission, the Welshes alone had seemed to enjoy the increased possibility for social life which the coming of the soldiers presented. Each night they played host to several men, and tonight was no exception. As she and Graham entered the cabin, Gloriana noticed two blue-coated soldiers still at the dinner table; the others had apparently just gotten up, for a harrassed-looking Mrs. Welsh was hurriedly clearing stacks of dirty dishes.

Bridgette Welsh was on a comfortable settee by the fireplace. Wearing a charming confection of light blue silk and playing off the attentions of the soldier sitting beside her against those of the soldier leaning over the back of the sofa, she seemed in her element. However, the welcome that had leaped to the girl's face when she saw Graham cooled perceptibly when she noticed who was with him.

But Mr. Welsh came forward with an expansive grin and a warm handshake and ushered them to a bench by the fire. His jollity puzzled Gloriana, for she had thought him an almost grim man; then she noticed the tankard in his hand and in those of the other men in the room. Suddenly she understood the almost unnatural air of hilarity in the cabin. To her amazement, sitting quietly by the fire were two of the younger men from the Klamath settlement. Their eyes seemed slightly glazed, as though they didn't see her, and by each of their sides was one of the large, pewter tankards.

"Miss Windemere, would you care to go upstairs to freshen up?" Bridgette asked sweetly after a moment. "You do look as though you took a tumble in the snow." Then her eyes spotted the traces of white on Graham Norton's broad back and the flakes in his hair.

"They look like they've both been rolling in the snow," one of the soldiers commented with a significant raise of his eyebrows that made the other guffaw coarsely.

Sensing the fury ready to erupt in Graham, Gloriana hurried ahead with her explanation of the Thanksgiving celebration. For once Bridgette seemed genuinely delighted, and she eagerly made promises for her family's contribution to the feast—promises which her father seconded heartily and to which her mother, in between trips to clear the table, assented with a meek smile.

Ordinarily Gloriana would have stayed to help that sad woman with the mountain of dishes that seemed to be her chore alone, but tonight she felt an urgent need to be out of that cabin with its artificial gaiety and undercurrents of domestic problems.

"I should have warned you about that place," Graham told her outside.

Gloriana tried to ignore the implication that he had spent enough evenings there to be well acquainted with the Welshes' social habits. "Does he always give drink to the Indians?"

"This is the first time I have seen it, but I doubt it will be the last. When the snows melt, Welsh plans to set up a trading post on his land claim. As far as I could see on the trip out, the only things he brought to trade were cases of whiskey."

Night had fallen and the sky shone with the cold, winking light of faraway stars. There was no moon, but the starlight reflected from the white snow with a shimmering glow. They crossed the wooded park at the center of the triangle. Even without their leaves the willows looked graceful and shapely, pale gray sentinels for the artesian spring. Amazingly the waters still bubbled and frothed, though ice had formed around the edge of the pond and snow covered the surrounding rocks.

They had paused a moment beside the spring when Gloriana felt Graham's hands on her shoulders turning her toward him. But instead of pulling her to him, Graham lifted her chin with a heavily gloved finger and tried to make her look at him.

"Glory, will you let me kiss you and admit that you

121

want to as much as I do, or do we have to go on pretending that I am stealing kisses from a very proper young miss?"

His words stung but his eyes were tender and compelling. He seemed to read the answer he wanted in her face, for when his cold lips touched and warmed against hers, the kiss was bolder and more demanding—the confident lovemaking of an accepted sweetheart. When after a moment her arms seemed to find their own way about his neck, Graham clasped her so tightly that Gloriana could barely breathe, and she tried to pull herself away with a shy laugh.

He let her go but only a few inches before he caught her back again. With his face pressed into the crown of curls at the top of her head, he breathed huskily, "Glory, darling, now what do you want to do about us?"

Us—Graham's voice lingered over the word, filling it with significance and magic, but warning signals were going off inside Gloriana's head.

"I need time to think," she faltered. He seemed disappointed but not overwhelmingly so.

"I've got to say this for your God," he said at last, smiling down at her. "He's finally done one good thing for me; He brought you here."

The words broke through the raptures of physical sensation to remind Gloriana of the barrier of faith between her and this man.

"Hasn't He ever done anything else for you?" she asked, not quite ready to start a discussion of their spiritual differences, yet curious all the same.

Graham, however, was unresponsive. Instead of answering, he began kissing her again, until he broke away with a shaky laugh and pleaded breathlessly, "Think, Glory, but don't think too long."

He held her carefully with his arm as they crossed the remaining yards to the Windemere cabin. Once he asked her if she was cold, and Gloriana discovered to her amazement that she was not; still she nodded that she was so that he would draw her closer. Another time they stopped to look toward the nearby lake, gleaming with the reflection of the silver starlight.

They had just realized that it was late, and neither had eaten dinner when a slim shadow darted out of the darkness and pulled them both urgently toward the cabin where Tildy and the Indian girls lived.

Even in the dim light, Gloriana could tell Oweena had been crying. "Don't speak. The lieutenant will hear," she whispered desperately. Gloriana and Graham exchanged a look filled with apprehension, then followed her as quietly as the crunching snow would allow.

Inside the cabin the lamps had been turned down, and the girls had pulled the curtains tightly. As Gloriana had half-begun to suspect, there was a still form lying on one of the beds. It took a full half-minute for Gloriana to recognize the proud Chief Keintepoos as the haggard warrior lying as though already dead.

"My land, girl, don't you know what the soldiers will do if they find him here?" Graham exclaimed as he too recognized the man.

"He was wounded in the fight, and there is infection. We must help," Oweena insisted, her agitated face showing the signs of nearing hysteria. The other girls crowded around them, adding their pleas.

"I'll get Uncle," Gloriana said at last.

"No!" He had seemed to be unconscious, but Keintepoos opened his eyes and spoke with surprising firmness. The broken body Gloriana hardly recognized, but the courageous spirit that looked out through those commanding eyes was that of the chief she remembered so well. And in spite of the attack on the soldiers, in spite of the rumors and accusations, she found herself once again trusting this man. He seemed to gather his strength, then went on with quiet dignity. "It is time for Keintepoos to die. I have come because Oweena is Christian. If I die without becoming Christian, we will go to different hunting grounds and our parting will be forever. I will take your Jesus path and go to heaven and wait for her there."

Tears rushed into Gloriana's eyes as she realized what the man was trusting her to do. Oweena had flung herself down beside the bed and, holding the chief's hand in both of hers, was sobbing. He spoke to her softly in their own tongue, then turned to Gloriana. "Keintepoos is ready."

But never had Gloriana felt less ready to lead a soul to Christ. Hadn't she just spent an hour behaving like a lovestruck schoolgirl with a man she knew was forbidden? Didn't she have some things to make right with her Saviour before she came to the Throne of Grace?

Perhaps this is what is meant by being "instant in season and out of season," Gloriana thought. Thanking God that the warrior knew English well and language would be no barrier, she began to tell him the greatest of all stories. When she came at last to the death on the cross, she saw the man's face soften with emotion, and she knew that whatever had been his original motives, Keintepoos had transcended them and believed. She remembered then that she had often questioned the sincerity of Oweena's Christian commitment, so she had her join hands with her sweetheart. Together they prayed a simple sinners' prayer that left Gloriana crying and, if she had but seen it, Graham Norton awed and shaken.

With the soul saved, the battle began to save the man's life. Graham had more experience with gunshot wounds than Gloriana, and he soon pronounced the problem to be a bullet embedded in the muscles of the right shoulder.

"For this we will need Uncle's medical bag at

least," Gloriana said and, bundling herself up, she hurried next door. To her dismay she found Lieutenant Tilton comfortably positioned on the sitting room couch, a heavy afghan wrapped around his legs, the only evidence of his invalid state.

"There you are, my dear. I was just telling the lieutenant about your excellent plan," her uncle halted her but, with a little apologetic smile, motioned to his back and did not rise. "A slight twinge of rheumatism," he called it, but Gloriana suspected the onset of arthritis.

"I've been spreading the word," she said with all the cheeriness she could muster. "The Midfields will contribute and also the Welshes. Oh, and Mr. Norton's men will supply venison and pheasants."

"Well, well! It's amazing what a pretty girl can accomplish in the space of a few hours, isn't it, Lieutenant?"

The officer agreed readily and lavished a few compliments on Gloriana's glowing cheeks and red lips. Then he added, "It will be good for the men to have something to occupy them for a day or two. For myself I prefer Christmas—especially since I hear the mistletoe grows abundantly in these forests." He looked meaningfully at Gloriana and laughed when the roses in her cheeks grew rosier.

At that moment Tildy came in and began to scold her for being late for dinner. All the while Gloriana was painfully aware that every second could mean the difference between Keintepoos's living or dying. Finally in desperation she drew her uncle aside and whispered that she needed his medical bag for some task in the next cabin. As she should have expected, the doctor insisted upon going himself, and Tildy demanded to know which of her girls was sick.

Feeling John Tilton's suddenly suspicious eyes on her, Gloriana cast around for a logical explanation.

"Is someone injured?" he demanded with a slight

edge to his voice that told her he was remembering the stories of Keintepoos and Chief John's kindness to the mission and already was forming a half-guess.

"If you must know," she burst out suddenly, "yes, there is something wrong. One of the Klamath girls has been attacked, and I seriously suspect one of your men of being responsible!"

Tilton looked startled, but she could see he believed her, and a fierce tension seemed to drain out of him with his suspicions. Her uncle and Tildy, however, were stunned. Both rushed for the cabin next door with stricken faces that said they somehow felt responsible for this calamity. They had barely gotten through the door before Dr. Windemere's repeated, "Shocking! Shocking!" changed to a businesslike, "Ah, I see." And he set to work.

CHAPTER 14

THE NEXT THREE DAYS, which had promised so much delightful diversion, became a nightmare. The mission bustled with the activities of preparation. The Thanksgiving feast would be held appropriately in the new meeting hall, and temporary tables of long, hand-hewn boards were being hastily erected on homemade sawhorses.

The young Welshes and some of the Klamaths took over decorating the partially finished hall, and soon the dirt floor was covered with sweet-scented wild hay. Shocks of Indian corn, colorful with their mixture of blue, black, yellow, and red kernels, adorned walls and the mantels of the huge open fireplace. Entire sheafs of dried cornstalks were brought in with the round golden pumpkins harvested earlier from Tildy's garden to fill the corners.

Through the bustle, the mission staff—all by now aware of the situation—hurried with bright smiles and troubled eyes. If the prayers at the morning services were a little more fervent than usual, observers put it down to the religious dimensions of the coming celebration or even to the missionaries' concern over the abused Indian girl.

Meant to be a profound secret, Gloriana's fabrication had spread quickly. Tensions had escalated between the workmen and the soldiers, threatening to disrupt the feast, until Lieutenant Tilton promised to find and punish the man. A delegation of wizened old men from the Klamath settlement had visited Dr. Windemere in protest and had to be let in on the secret. And Tildy scolded Gloriana soundly for ruining her credibility as a chaperone and guardian of her girls.

Fortunately, Gloriana had not mentioned a name, although she strongly suspected that none of the girls, including Oweena, would have minded slandering one of the bluecoats. She held firmly to this refusal, in spite of the lieutenant's protest that he needed to question the girl so that he could begin looking for the attacker.

Meanwhile Keintepoos fought for his life in one cabin while a few yards away Lieutenant Tilton regained his strength.

The lieutenant was a problem. Leaning on a cane, he managed to find his way to every room in the Windemere cabin, particularly if Gloriana was there. And she, remembering that he had thirty-nine able men at the mission and a legitimate reason for hating Keintepoos, appeared kinder than she felt.

"What is a lovely thing like you doing in a place like this?"

Gloriana, on her knees in the storeroom, turned and tried to summon a smile. She had been looking for a precious jar of nutmeg that Tildy needed for the pumpkin pies and had not heard John Tilton enter, but still she was not surprised to find him hovering behind her. With a lopsided bandage around his head and leaning heavily on his makeshift cane, he looked vulnerable, and a flashing smile added an almost boyish charm to his features. Yet Gloriana could not escape the feeling of menace whenever she was near him.

"You are a flatterer, Lieutenant," she forced a light, teasing tone. "In this old housedress and with my hair bound in a rag, I can hardly be called lovely."

"But to her most devoted admirer, Cinderella is merely in disguise," Tilton responded gallantly and offered a hand to help her to her feet.

She accepted reluctantly, then wished she had not as his hand grasped hers with surprising energy.

"What a crime it is to bury a glorious creature like you in the wilderness." He still held onto her hand, and the warmth in his eyes was unmistakable.

"How silly! Nobody is burying me here. I chose to come."

But he went on as though he had not heard her, "You should be dressed in silks and satins and spend your days gossiping and drinking tea and your nights dancing and flirting."

Gloriana snatched her hand away impatiently and tried to slip past him to the door. The tiny room was dark and close, and the musty odors of dust and stagnant air mingled with the more pleasant smells of spices and drying fruit. The ceiling-high shelves that lined the walls were stuffed full of jars, tins, and sacks—an effective barrier against sound, and the door, which the lieutenant had nearly closed behind him, admitted only a thin ribbon of light.

"I could make all that happen for you," Tilton said softly, but there was nothing soft or gentle about the hand that grasped her shoulder or the body that pressed her back against the shelf.

Fighting the impulse to struggle, Gloriana summoned a little laugh that she hoped did not sound too nervous. "You could also make me drop this jar of nutmeg, for which neither Tildy nor the pumpkin pies will thank you." She forced herself to smile at him, though the man's closeness chilled her.

His answering smile was tight-lipped, and heavily lidded eyes hid their expression from her in the half-light. "All right," he said finally, "I'll play along for now. But let's hope, my dear Miss Windemere, that your stand-offishness is caused by maidenly modesty, not by some deeper game you're playing." His fingers tightened on Gloriana's arm until she winced, but his smile did not vary, and his voice sank to an even softer, hissing whisper. "Because if you are, the consequences will not be pleasant."

He let her go then, and Gloriana bolted from the room, forgetting to maintain her air of studied nonchalance. The lieutenant's mild threat, delivered in smooth, well-oiled tones, had frightened her more than an angry warning might have. She would have to be more careful. And underlying her terror was the certainty that they were playing a very deep game indeed, and none of the missionaries, she least of all, fully understood all that was involved.

Tildy looked at her oddly as Gloriana delivered the nutmeg, then glanced behind the girl at the limping officer.

"Auntie, will you let me lick the frosting bowl?" John Tilton began teasing, his voice as light and his smile as charming as ever.

"I'm not your aunt, young man," Tildy snapped testily and took a swat at his hand which was reaching for one of the giant round cookies she was frosting. But she made room for him on one of the long benches and gave him a bowl with enough frosting left on its sides to thrill the heart of any youngster.

Gloriana watched them from the corner of her eye as she began to roll out the pie crust. It was difficult to find much menace in the man who was teasing her uncle's housekeeper and scraping every lick of frosting from the bowl as gleefully as a child. Perhaps it was her own guilty conscience that colored his words with so much danger. But once or twice she thought she felt his eyes on her half-turned back and a little tremor ran through her.

"Miss Gloriana, if you keep rolling that crust, it will fill two pie tins," Tildy's sharp tone recalled Gloriana to her work, and she looked down to see that she had absently rolled an oblong instead of a neat circle.

"I'm sorry, Tildy," she murmured hastily and, folding the pastry in half, lifted it gingerly into a plate where it drooped over two sides, leaving bare half moons of pie tin between. She heard Tildy sniff skeptically as she pared off the excess and tried to piece it over the bare spots.

"You young men! Always turning a girl's head and making her useless in the kitchen," Tildy scolded John Tilton.

He did not seem to mind the hint that he had somehow "turned" Gloriana's head but laughed delightedly. "I'll bet Gloriana had a lot of beaus back in Philadelphia," he suggested.

"Gloriana? No, she spent all of her time tagging after her doctor uncle or doctoring birds and sick kittens in her pet hospital. But Miss Juliana and Miss Marianna—now there was honey that attracted the bees!" And with the perfect familiarity of a long-time family member, Tildy began to tell about the romances of Gloriana's more popular sisters. Only half listening, Gloriana missed the point when the conversation turned back to herself.

"Miss Gloriana is a good, serious-minded girl," Tildy was scolding again. "You young jackanapes should leave her be. Do your sparkin' with them that's lookin' for it, like that little Bridgette Welsh. Now there's some honey that goes looking for the bees."

Gloriana smiled. Dear Tildy! She did not miss a thing! And she had come up with the perfect solution if only John Tilton would follow her advice. Bridgette and the volatile lieutenant would be perfectly matched—he with his insincere charm and she with her insincere sweetness.

But if the lieutenant heard the suggestion, he paid no attention. Instead of questioning Tildy about Bridgette, he asked, "What other young jackanapes are you warning away, Auntie?" His voice sounded pleasant enough, but there was a slight edge to it that made Gloriana hold her breath as she willed Tildy to say nothing.

Tildy, however, seemed to be warming to the subject. "Well, there's that nice Graham Norton and, of course, you heard about Chief John offering for her." Lieutenant Tilton had not heard, and to Gloriana's horror, Tildy told him the entire story, embellishing it in a way that made her pride in Gloriana clear as well as the great friendship that had developed between the warrior and the mission staff.

"Well, well, Norton and Chief John," he said when she had finished. "I can't think of any two rivals that I would more enjoy beating." And catching Gloriana's glance, he gave her a smile that would have been more dazzling if it had reached his eyes.

She wanted to tell him that he had no chance of beating anyone, but she knew she could not. Keintepoos, Oweena, the Klamaths, the Mission—all would remain safe, she knew instinctively, only so long as she and the others played their parts. They were missionaries, and deception did not come naturally to them. How much longer they would be able to play the game, she had no idea, yet she had little doubt of the consequences if they did not play it well.

That they could be in danger from the very men who should be protecting them seemed incredible. Gloriana remembered her brother at West Point, so idealistic and proud in his cadet uniform, and her father's older brother, Colonel Robert Windemere, whose sweeping whiskers and deep laugh always made her think of Santa Claus. In the East the military

132

had been a symbol of all that was secure and grand about her world, but here in Oregon Territory these men in blue uniforms reminded her of nothing so much as Keintepoos and Chief John's band of warriors—wild, powerful, and free, capable of great good but also of great harm. And of the two bands, the soldiers or the Indians, Gloriana felt at this moment that she would more readily trust herself to the Indians.

"Keep your fingers out of those cookies, and I am not your auntie!" Tildy was again scolding the young officer. His laughter as he teased the cranky housekeeper sounded as lighthearted as that of any of her brother's West Point friends, and Gloriana could tell that in spite of her grumbling, Tildy was enjoying his nonsense.

You're making too much of some idle threats, Gloriana told herself, but still she could not shake the feeling of apprehension and enter into the light banter. When Dr. Windemere came to take her on his afternoon rounds, she was eager to escape the house.

"I'm sorry to take away your star pie maker," Gloriana heard Uncle Ralph apologize as she hurried for her cloak. Tildy did not say anything, but her loud "hmmph!" made clear her opinion of Gloriana's pie making for that day at least.

Outside a wet snow was falling. Giant flakes floated lazily on the cold, heavy air, smothering sound. A peaceful hush submerged the distant clamor of hammers and saws as men worked in the new chapel to prepare it for the following day's festivities. On the hillside beneath the schoolhouse some of the children were tobogganing in what looked like giant baskets made of reeds. Excited dogs were chasing the children to the bottom of the slope, but the happy noises of barking and laughing were a faraway murmur.

Picking her way along the half-hidden path beside her uncle, Gloriana relaxed, for what seemed like the first time in hours.

"I think Tildy was getting ready to send me to my room for ruining so many of her pies," she confided to her uncle with a little giggle.

He patted her mittened hand where it rested in the crook of his arm and smiled briefly but did not comment. The rosy old face was nearly buried behind a knitted red cap and muffler, and a thick mask of white beard and bushy eyebrows caught the snowflakes and held them in a wet fringe. Gloriana thought affectionately how like an old elf he looked and realized how much she had missed him since he had left Philadelphia. How glad she was, in spite of the hardships and the dangers, that she had answered his call to Oregon Territory!

"How is our patient?" she prompted gently, trying to prod him out of an abstraction that she feared might look odd to any suspicious viewers.

The old doctor looked startled for a moment, then patting her hand again said reassuringly, "He has a chance, a fighting chance." He would not say any more but, as though his mind were made up about something, steered her determinedly toward the hospital.

On the covered walkway that served as a hospital entrance, they hit their heavy boots against the steps to dislodge the snow, and Gloriana shook the voluminous folds of her cape as well to keep from tracking in any more dampness than necessary.

She never stepped inside this frontier hospital without conflicting emotions. While impressed by what her uncle had accomplished, Gloriana could not help comparing the frontier hospital with the gleaming wards and sparkling operating rooms of the hospitals back home. There the wounds that still held a few of the soldiers to their beds would have been minor afflictions rather than the life-threatening crises they were out here.

"Someday on this spot I will build a three-story

modern hospital," Dr. Windemere said quietly, as though he had read her mind or perhaps seen the same comparisons in his own mind. "Or perhaps your children will have to build it for me." He gave her an odd little half-smile and motioned the way toward his office.

Completely mystified, Gloriana led the way, but once inside the little cubicle, her unpredictable uncle demanded tea. The hot brew had been prepared and was sitting before them in the chipped white shaving mugs that the doctor always kept for that purpose before he would resume.

Ralph Windemere leaned back in his chair and smiled fondly at his niece. "Gloriana, my dear, I think you know how much I have appreciated your being here. I did not think to see any of my own family again, let alone have someone of my own to carry on after I am gone."

"Uncle, what is wrong? Have the soldiers . . .?"

Ralph Windemere held up a hand and shook his head. "Let me finish. I know I am making a mess of this, but you will have to forgive an old man who loves you . . . Gloriana, do you want to stay here? Is your heart with these people and this land of mine?"

Was it? Gloriana dug into herself for a moment, wondering. She had come to Oregon Territory because she wanted to help her uncle and because she believed in the mission—that was true. But it was also true that she had come because life back home in Philadelphia had ceased to have much meaning, because she was tired of the church socials and picnics and tired too of being the older, sensible Windemere sister. Here on the frontier she had found not only meaningful work and excitement, but also a way to make her life count.

"Yes, Uncle, I will stay," she said finally with a calm she was far from feeling.

Dr. Windemere nodded, as though she had said

what he had expected, but Gloriana could tell from the way he reached for his pipe and began absently to fill the bowl that he was nervous.

"Uncle, has something gone wrong? Is there anything I can do?"

Again he held up his hand and motioned impatiently for her to let him continue. "Now, Gloriana, this is hard enough for me without your interrupting. I'm trying to do this the way I think my brother—your father—would want it done." He paused for a moment to try to light the pipe, sucking in through the stem and filling his face with little clouds of smoke while she looked on in increasingly agitated fascination. But she did not try to hurry him again. After a moment he gave up on the pipe and set it down, still unlit.

"I could not discuss this at home because I was afraid our houseguest might make things awkward. Am I right in saying, my dear, that Lieutenant Tilton has more than a passing interest in you?"

"But I have no interest whatsoever in him, Uncle!"

The doctor smiled at the energy of her answer, but he could not resist teasing, "He's a very handsome young man. I should think he would set all of the young ladies' hearts to beating faster."

"Not mine," she said with a little shudder and told him about the threat.

Dr. Windemere looked grim but not surprised. "It's difficult to keep power responsive to the people when it is nearly independent of supervision. The nearest regular army post is at Winnemucca, nearly two hundred miles away.

"Besides, I'm afraid the lieutenant may be doing exactly what his orders say—patrolling and searching for that band of so-called renegades. If he found the chief here, I'm afraid he might be well within his rights to charge us with obstructing justice and retaliate."

"What would they do to Keintepoos if they found him?"

"Hang him—or worse yet, imprison him on some army post chained up like an animal in a box where all could see him."

The mental picture of the proud warrior held up to the mockery and even the pity of his former foes overruled Gloriana's well-trained Eastern conscience; perhaps they were obstructing justice but certainly that was justifiable to avoid an even greater injustice. Still, was Lieutenant Tilton being unjust? He and his men had been brutally attacked; several had been killed; many, injured. And no one, not even Oweena, had claimed that Keintepoos and Chief John were innocent.

"We must face it," mused her uncle, whose thoughts had apparently been following the same course as her own. "It could be better for all of us if our gallant chief does not survive."

"But, Oweena . . .!" Gloriana started to protest.

"I know, I know. The child would be heartbroken, but at least she is assured of being with him in the next life, if not in this."

They sat for a few minutes without speaking, forgetting to drink their tea. Their eyes rested absently on the doctor's desk lamp. It was smoking slightly, and a thin film of carbon on the glass dimmed the light so that in the tightly shuttered office, there seemed to be a perpetual twilight. It would have made an attractive painting—the old doctor and his young nurse, their sad expressions and drooping shoulders suggesting a shared but nonetheless heavy burden. Both realized that by the laws of the civilization they both believed in, they were harboring a fugitive. But just as surely the laws of a higher kingdom and their healing profession required them to care for the injured and provide refuge to those who claimed it in God's name. Moreover, the man was a friend to whom they owed much.

"At least through all this, Keintepoos has been brought to Christ—and Oweena, too," Gloriana said finally. The memory of the glowing wonder in the Indian couple's eyes as they realized the Savior's love for them eased some of the anxiety she was feeling.

Her uncle brightened at that. "What a breakthrough it would give us with these people if we could tell them about Keintepoos! So far our successes have come with the old or the very young or with the women. This would give us a chance to show the men that the Jesus way, as they call it, is for warriors too." He paused a moment and looked speculatively at his niece. "We have already had some success in that direction."

A slight note of excitement in her uncle's voice made Gloriana lean forward expectantly, but she was hardly prepared for what he said next.

"Graham Norton came to me last night. He was deeply moved by Keintepoos's desire to be with Oweena in the next world and by the way you led the chief to Christ. He asked me if it would be just as easy for a prodigal son to get back on the right path.

"It seems he has been a very bitter man where God is concerned. Losing his parents at such a young age when they were working for the Lord appeared to convince him that God was unfair and did not care about him. I think our Indian chief helped him to get a different perspective on Christianity, showed him it is a walk, a pathway leading somewhere and convinced him that he might not have given God a chance in his life."

"He said I was the one good thing God had done for him," Gloriana murmured half to herself.

"Hmmm . . . yes. I understood you were becoming involved, but I had no idea how far things had gone. As your nearest relative out here on the frontier, Graham spoke to me about his feelings for you. Gloriana, I have to stand in the place of your father to

138

you in this, and that means I have a responsibility. I believe Graham cares for you very deeply, and I think he is one of the finest men I have ever known. As a Christian he will be a giant, a man to match this empire-sized country, able to make it everything we pioneers and missionaries dream about.

"But, my dear, he made one thing very clear. If you choose to make your life with him, you will have to do it here in the West. It's possible you will never be able to go back home again."

Dr. Windemere picked up his pipe and began absently to empty and refill it. The strain of balancing his own wishes against what he felt he owed his niece and his absent brother showed in the round, usually jovial face. A few drops of moisture showed on the red cheeks, and he brushed them away hastily with the back of his hand.

"I asked you a few minutes ago whether you plan to stay here and you said yes. Nothing would make me happier than to spend the rest of my years with my dear niece and her family nearby. You know, Gloriana, that you have always been to me the child I never had—from the times you used to pester me to doctor your sick animals until now when you answered my call for a nurse.

"But I want you to be absolutely certain that the West and Graham Norton are what you want. Search your heart, pray about it, and be sure before you make your decision."

It would be several hours before Gloriana would have a chance to follow her uncle's advice.

CHAPTER 15

GLORIANA HURRIED through the rest of her day, feeling something like one of the wind-up toys she had found under the Christmas tree as a child. There was much to do, and she moved quickly from duty to duty. Yet it was as though her spirit were elsewhere. She felt she should be happy. The major barrier between her and Graham Norton was gone. He was now a Christian, and he sought her hand in the accepted way—by declaring his intentions to her nearest male relative and stating what he had to offer.

"My prayers have been answered," she reminded herself, yet she could not escape a little feeling of disappointment that chilled her inside as the wet snow soaking through the shoulders of her cloak and dampening the hem of her skirt chilled her outside. Graham had placed a condition on his love. That it was a condition she would and could meet made little difference. There was an "if" in the man's feelings for her.

"You're a hopeless romantic," she scolded herself and tried to remember that there had been an "if" on her side as well: if he had not accepted Christ, she could not have accepted Graham, no matter how she felt. *I must look at the half of the cup that is full,* Gloriana thought. *We are adults. We can't be expected to "give all for love" like a pair of love-struck youngsters.* Still she could not help envying Oweena whose sweetheart had given up his Happy Hunting Grounds, as he thought, to be with her in heaven. That Oweena stood a good chance of losing Keintepoos either did not occur to her, or at least did not alter her own vague feelings of discontent.

She was truly thankful that Keintepoos's example had moved Graham to return to the faith of his fathers. She was truly thankful that she had found someone in the great West that she could admire and look up to. And she was thankful that her uncle approved of the match.

"So why am I complaining?" She would see Graham, and after the first awkwardness of accepting him was over, then she would feel happy. And perhaps she could even get him to retract that condition, to promise to take her back East if that was what she wanted. *As Lieutenant Tilton offered to do,* the thought came unbidden before she dismissed it angrily. But try as she might she could not dismiss the odd feeling of discontent that made her prayers of thanks perfunctory at best and diluted them with a string of postscripts that seemed more concerned with adding instructions for accomplishing future answers than with expressing appreciation for the answers that had come.

"Glory, wait!" Graham Norton's familiar voice broke into Gloriana's train of thought with a suddenness that left her bewildered for a moment. The snow had stopped falling, and the path she was following across the mission yard had been recently shoveled. Overhead the sun was just visible—a round, muted light through thinning layers of white clouds.

Graham's glad smile as he caught up with her was reassuring, while the eager light in his blue eyes made it difficult to meet his gaze. And suddenly Gloriana was aware of being in the center of the mission yard, overlooked by a dozen windows and perhaps watched by half of the mission's population.

Graham reached for the medical bag Gloriana was carrying and then for her mittened hand which he tucked possessively in the crook of his arm.

"Did Dr. Windemere tell you?" he asked with such a tender expression that Gloriana's heart turned over in her chest, even though her mind was crying, *Not here! Not now!*

But for once Graham did not read Gloriana's expression accurately, and he pressed ahead with all the confidence of someone who knows the answer but wants it confirmed. "Well, what did you decide? Will you stay—with me?"

She would have liked to have put off answering him, but there was no denying his air of urgency and eagerness. Still looking at the large, gloved hand that encompassed her small mittened one, Gloriana nodded briefly. She felt his cold lips brush quickly against her cheek; then he laughed with a mixture of embarrassment and jubilation.

"I can't show you here how I really feel," he said huskily, and Gloriana wondered if he had just then noticed their lack of privacy. He pulled off his glove and reached into his pocket. Gloriana felt something cold and hard slip inside her mitten.

"Wear that," the man told her with a grin that made him look rather young and foolish, and her heart began to warm to the happiness that radiated from Graham's face. His red-gold curls fell from under his hat across his still summer-bronzed forehead. The sky-blue eyes that Gloriana had seen spark with anger or harden to mask his feelings, glowed warmly through a thick fringe of gold lashes. His smile

142

softened the hard set of his jaw and completed the thawing of Gloriana's heart.

"It will be a good life," Graham said softly, "and we'll have God in our home."

Gloriana had started to tell him as well as to feel herself how happy his coming to Christ had made her when she was interrupted by a high-pitched call. Tripping through the snow was Bridgette Welsh. Dressed all in light blue wool, her head and hands daintily clad in immaculate white fur, she looked ready for a Sunday skating party. She was carrying a large basket which appeared to grow heavier as she approached Graham and Gloriana.

"Oh, Mr. Norton, I'm so glad I caught you," Bridgette breathed a sigh and gave him her sweetest smile. "Could you help me carry this heavy basket to the chapel? Momma and I have been baking all day, and I find I am just not strong enough to carry everything."

Gloriana glanced at Graham to see how he was responding to Bridgette's clinging-vine act and was pleased to see a look of annoyance on his face. However, he reached for the basket and allowed the girl to take his arm.

"Couldn't you come with us?" he appealed to Gloriana, but she shook her head. "Then come to the chapel later and see our preparations for tomorrow." She promised that she would and, taking back her medical bag, tried not to see the look of triumph in the glance Bridgette flung in her direction.

"Dear Miss Windemere, so dedicated and so competent," Gloriana heard Bridgette gushing as the vision in blue drew Graham away. Gloriana wanted to say that the basket would not have seemed so heavy if Bridgette had not carried it a hundred yards out of her way so that she could waylay Graham. She wanted to suggest that Momma and not Bridgette had probably done all of the cooking. And most of all, she wanted to tell Bridgette that Graham had asked her—the dedicated, competent spinster—to be his wife.

But she did not say any of those things. Instead she stood quietly watching her fiancé of less than five minutes trying to evade the clinging Bridgette Welsh and maintain a respectable distance as he carried her basket toward the large log chapel.

I can't believe this is happening to me, Gloriana told herself, half exasperated and half amused. *I just accepted the proposal of a man who says he will marry me only if I agree to live in the West, a man who forces me to give my answer in a public place with dozens of people watching and then walks away with a blonde on his arm two minutes after I say yes. I must be out of my mind.*

She sighed and resumed her walk along the snow-packed path. She felt the hard circular shape of the ring Graham had slipped inside her mitten. *I even get to put on my own engagement ring. No romantic moonlight or whispered vows or breathless kisses. Just, "Here's a ring and I'll see you later."* By the time she reached Oweena's cabin, Gloriana was thoroughly angry with Graham and just as thoroughly disgusted with herself.

Before I marry that man, he will ask me properly when we're alone and there's no Bridgette Welsh around, and . . . he'll say, "I love you"! she vowed silently, conveniently forgetting that she had already agreed to marry Graham and retracting her promise would be decidedly awkward.

In the meantime there was work to be done. Keintepoos would need his wounds looked to, and to avoid suspicion, Dr. Windemere had sent Gloriana alone to change the dressings and report on the warrior's progress. "No one will think it odd if you visit your friend," the doctor had told her, "but they might become suspicious if I go there too often. I will slip over later tonight after our houseguest has gone to sleep."

Oweena's room was dark and quiet. As Gloriana opened the door, she felt the hush of sickness hanging in the air. Oweena, who had been kneeling beside the bed, ran to hug Gloriana, and the wetness of her friend's cheek told Gloriana better than words the condition of the patient.

Keintepoos lay very still, his massive frame dwarfing the small bed. His pulse was weak and his temperature, high.

"What have you done to bring down the fever?" Gloriana asked. Oweena showed her the wet cloths and basin of water by the bed.

"Dr. Ralph said to change these every ten minutes." There was also chamomile tea, but the man's teeth were clenched and he had taken none in hours.

"We must get his temperature down. Go out the back door where you will not be seen, and fill this basin with snow." And Gloriana set to work with a will, her own problems forgotten in the greater troubles of the Indian chief.

The wounds were many, and most were infected. As she washed them carefully and applied fresh dressings, Gloriana marveled that the man was still alive. It had been weeks since the battle, and many of the soldiers, who had been treated within days of the conflict, were only now beginning to recover. How he had survived so long in the open she had no idea. She wondered briefly what had happened to Chief John and the other warriors. Tilton had insisted that the Indians had wiped out his fort as well as an entire village, yet the presence of Keintepoos alone and near death at the mission suggested defeat rather than victory.

There was some mystery here and the only ones who could explain it were Keintepoos, who could not speak, and the soldiers, who would not. Gloriana remembered her talk a few hours before with her uncle and his regretful comment that perhaps they would all be better off if the chief did not survive.

"Lord, help us," she breathed the prayer, encompassing in three simple words her anxieties about harboring a fugitive and the deeper feeling, an intuition born nearer the heart than the head, that the survival of this Indian chief was somehow essential to the life and safety of all of them.

Ordinarily Gloriana would have watched and prayed with a patient like Keintepoos throughout the night, but she dared not stay long for fear someone would become suspicious. She showed Oweena how to apply the snow packs and thought she felt the first signs of the fever's breaking in the man's burning skin. Then with an encouraging hug and the promise that she would pray, Gloriana left the Indian girls to fight the battle alone.

It was twilight outside, and Gloriana realized with a little feeling of panic that she had stayed with Keintepoos longer than she realized. Soon it would be dinnertime, and if she was too late, she would be missed and questions would be asked.

I could say there is sickness—maybe whooping cough—in the Indian village, she thought and as quickly rejected the idea. What if the lieutenant had his soldiers watching her? They would know that it had been hours since she had visited the Klamath village and there might even be one of those young braves she had seen at the Welsh cabin who would know that she had only lanced a boil and checked on the progress of roasting venison and firepit baked apaws that were being prepared for the following day.

"Whoever said the liar's way is the easy way has never tried it. Deception is hard work."

The half-finished chapel was lit only by fires in the fireplaces and a single lamp on one of the long makeshift tables. It smelled delightfully of hay and wood shavings and burning wood. The young people's decorations looked almost exotic in the half-light, and for a moment Gloriana was reminded of Thanksgiv-

146

ings back home with church suppers and the Pilgrims' play done by the Sunday sschool classes. The memory made her suddenly homesick and she realized how much she longed to hear her father's deep voice singing "We Thank Thee, O God" and her sister Juliana's rippling accompaniment, always a bit too fast with too many trills and arpeggios for a hymn.

To her surprise she saw that someone had moved the organ from the old chapel and set it in the place of honor on a half-completed platform. The pulpit was there, too—all ready with a pitcher of water and a glass at the side for the Thanksgiving sermon Uncle Ralph had been chewing on for days. Very little was left to be done. The tables groaned with baskets of food and stacks of dishes. Kettles and pots waited beside the fireplaces to begin the work of warming food and brewing the mixture of coffee and grains that would be a special treat for the occasion.

There was every evidence of a day's hard work on preparations for the feast but no evidence of the workers. *He didn't even wait*, Gloriana thought and smiled somewhat grimly. She supposed that being stood up was on a par with the rest of the events of her engagement day, but that did not make it any easier to swallow. Perhaps Graham had decided she was not coming. Perhaps he had gone to find her at the cabin and was even now hurrying across the mission yard. In any case, he did not seem to be in the chapel.

Gloriana had just turned to leave when she heard a sound from the direction of the platform. She had forgotten about the small room that was being built there for a church office. Thinking that Graham must have decided to do some work in the little room while he waited for her, Gloriana hurried forward. It did not occur to her to call out.

But what she saw in the shadows on the other side of the door made her heart stop—a man and a woman

147

locked together in an embrace. Even in the dim light the red hair and broad shoulders of Graham Norton and the pale yellow curls of Bridgette Welsh were unmistakable.

Gloriana's gasp startled the pair, and for one breathless moment she looked straight into Graham's horrified face. Then Gloriana ran from the chapel. Behind her she heard Graham's frantic, "Glory, wait!" and the girl's high-pitched laughter.

Dry-eyed, but hardly seeing where she was going, Gloriana ran along the slippery path. Twice she fell, the second time with her arm beneath her. She felt a sharp pain in her left wrist, but she picked herself up and ran on. She could hardly realize what had happened. She felt as though she were caught in a night terror—one of those senseless dreams where one runs blindly, pursued by some indescribable horror. But in her mind she carried with her a vivid picture of two faces pressed tightly together—a picture she could not leave behind nor shut out, not even by closing her eyes.

CHAPTER 16

Oregon Territory   November 26, 1851
Thanksgiving

We celebrated our first Thanksgiving in the wilderness today and I am homesick. I miss my mother's turkey and cranberries and my father's impossibly long blessing over the food. I even miss seeing Juliana's latest gentleman friend—probably another cadet from West Point or perhaps a student from the university this year. She always invites someone to dinner and then introduces him as though he were "the one," only to pick someone different the next year.

Our celebration here was a success, according to Uncle—there were no fights. The soldiers and Graham Norton's men sat at opposite ends of the room with the Klamaths in between. Uncle's sermon was well received, though he looked very tired to me. I doubt he slept at all last night.

I could not play the organ. My left wrist, injured when I fell last night, is swollen and bruised. Catherine Midfield played, and from the feeling she put into the old hymns, I think she must be as homesick as I.

Gloriana would not let her mind go over the events of the day before, but she could not escape the aching emptiness they had left inside her. She had not spoken to Graham since she had seen him with Bridgette in the chapel, though he had called at the cabin several times and sent notes asking to see her. Her pride had willed her to act as though nothing had happened, but her acting ability had not been equal to the task. For once, she was glad that Lieutenant Tilton stuck close to her; still dazed, she had appreciated his help with filling her plate at the Thanksgiving feast and his constant stream of small talk, in spite of her silence. She was not, however, so numb that she missed the puzzled looks the Midfields exchanged or her uncle's sober expression as he watched her. Nor was she completely unaware of Graham Norton's anxious eyes on her and his increasing anger at Tilton's attentions. Finally, Graham had left his place of honor near her uncle to sit farther down the table with a delighted Bridgette Welsh.

"I don't care!" Gloriana said sharply, but not very convincingly.

A few minutes later a soft knock at the bedroom door made Gloriana hastily wipe away a few tears that had somehow found their way down her cheeks.

Her uncle stood at her doorway, spectacles on his nose and medical bag in hand. "Let's take a look at that wrist," he said, after a quick inspection of the bruise on her cheek. If he noticed the rice powder she had used to try to cover it or the little streaks left by her recent tears, he said nothing but went right to work on her wrist, probing and feeling with sure fingers.

"There's nothing broken," he said finally, then added with a keen look into her eyes, "at least nothing in your hand. I'm not so sure about the rest of you." Little by little, he drew from her the story of what had happened the day before. When she had finished and fresh tears were rolling down her cheeks, he was frowning and shaking his head.

"I don't understand it. I have known Graham Norton for several years, and what you tell me does not sound like him at all."

"But I saw him, Uncle! In the chapel behind the platform. And today he was with her again."

"Did he have no explanation? Could she have stumbled and fallen and he caught her? Or might she have thrown herself on him? She seems like a rather forward young woman—not at all above putting a man in a difficult situation."

Gloriana shook her head skeptically, but she had to admit that she had not waited for Graham's explanation.

"Well, he will have to explain to me," her uncle said decidedly.

Gloriana, however, insisted she did not want anything worked out and, when her uncle left, she gave him the beautiful ruby ring Graham had pressed into her mitten—could it only have been the afternoon before? It seemed much longer ago.

"That does not look like the kind of ring a man would give a girl he is two-timing," Dr. Windemere commented, but he put the ring in his waistcoat pocket. Gloriana could still hear him arguing with himself as he went downstairs, and she felt almost as sorry for the trusting old doctor as she did for herself.

If Gloriana's world had turned suddenly gray, it had not been frozen. The work at the mission went on. New babies continued to be born in the Klamath village, sick children had to be nursed, and the conspiracy of silence over the wounded Shasta chief had to be maintained. The attacks by the renegades had begun once again—closer now, it seemed, to the mission. The party of a British lord, wintering a few miles north, had been saved by a band of hunters from the mission, but not before they had been robbed of a considerable quantity of gold and jewels.

There was plenty to occupy Gloriana's time and her

mind, and since she had never been given to gloom and self-pity, she soon threw herself into her duties with an energy that could not fail to be rewarded. If her smiles were not quite as ready as before, if she felt a sharp pain in her heart when some chance incident reminded her that that organ existed, it was only to be expected. "Time heals all wounds," she reminded herself, "or at least teaches us to bear them patiently."

She never knew what her uncle said to Graham Norton. The relationship between the old doctor and his young friend seemed as cordial as ever when they met around the mission yard or in his office—a fact that Gloriana tried not to resent too much. Yet Norton no longer came to the Windemere cabin for evenings of talk and pipe smoking.

Surprisingly he was usually in church, sometimes with Bridgette Welsh beside him, sometimes alone. Back at her place at the organ, Gloriana would sense his entry into the chapel before she caught sight of his broad shoulders and uncovered head of red curls. He usually sat in the back row, but he towered nearly head and shoulders above the congregation, mostly made up of Klamaths, with only a few of the other mission inhabitants mixed in. When Bridgette was with him, Gloriana had to steel herself to endure the service. Then the organ seemed possessed of an evil spirit that pressed the wrong keys, made the rhythm of her pumping irregular, and caused the instrument to wheeze awkwardly.

When he was alone, she felt intensely self-conscious, wondering if he was watching her and hoping that he could not feel her awareness of him. Her quick ear even picked out his deep baritone voice in the singing. Her every sense seemed attuned to this man who had hurt her so badly, yet for all the sign he gave, he might not have known she was there.

Meanwhile Keintepoos continued to hang between

life and death. Most of the wounds closed and began to heal, but a deep one near his left lung refused to respond to treatment.

"If I had him back home in a modern hospital, I know I could handle it, but here. . ." Dr. Windemere shook his head. His round, white-fringed face showed as much discouragement as Gloriana had ever seen there.

"Someday you'll have your modern hospital right here," she reminded him, but for once the dream did not bring a light to the doctor's eyes nor start him talking about the better times to come.

"Perhaps," was all he answered.

They had met once again in Gloriana's tiny room—the only place in the cabin where they did not have to worry about John Tilton's walking in or overhearing their conversation. Dr. Windemere was resting in her rocking chair, one hand holding his unlit pipe; the other, absently rubbing the smooth wood of the scrolled arm. Gloriana sat on the edge of the bed, a knitted comforter wrapped tightly around her to keep out the chill of the unheated room.

"I'm afraid the lieutenant is becoming suspicious," she told her uncle after a moment. "He keeps asking me about Oweena and why she isn't helping in the hospital any more."

"What did you tell him?"

"I said she was pining for her Indian sweetheart and gushed a lot about how romantic it was."

"Was he convinced?"

"I don't think so, at least not entirely. I'm not sure how much longer we can keep putting him off. I have a feeling that already he is trying to get a look inside that cabin."

The doctor hesitated and cleared his throat, then spoke. "Graham suggests moving Keintepoos to the Midfields' cabin. Then he would have a doctor with him day and night, and he would be out of Tilton's way.

Gloriana tried to keep the tremor from her voice at the mention of Graham, but she knew she was hiding nothing from her kindly and observant uncle. "When and how could it be done?"

"At night when everyone is asleep."

Two nights later, instead of taking an indirect route around the back of the cabins, Graham and his men carried the wonded chief straight across the mission yard. There was no moon, but stars and snow made the night bright enough that the men and the stretcher were visible. Gloriana watched from the open window of her room, wondering how many other eyes followed them. The scuffling sounds their feet made on the snow-packed path were insignificant in the comparison to the sharp cracking noise of boots' breaking through frozen snow crust that Gloriana had expected to hear.

In the days that followed Gloriana escaped more and more into her work. With the lieutenant seeming to be everywhere in the Windemere cabin, she found the hospital a refuge. The medications she had to prepare kept her mind busy, and the appreciation of the patients made her feel that she was doing something worthwhile.

It was less than a week before Christmas, and the hospital ward looked more cheerful than she felt. A fire crackled merrily in the closed stove—one of the few at the mission. Paper chains and snowflakes decorated the windows, and a large fir tree stood in the coolness near the door. Handmade ornaments of cloth and painted wood covered the green branches, and on top a five-pointed star, cut from tin, shone brightly.

Back home they would be shopping and wrapping presents. Juliana would be practicing Christmas carols on the old upright piano in the living room while Marianna altered Wise Men's robes and angel costumes for another generation of Sunday-school pupils who would be performing in the annual Christmas Eve pageant.

"I wonder if they miss me," Gloriana asked, unconsciously speaking aloud.

"Not half as much as we would if you weren't here." The unexpected answer coming from close by made Gloriana jump, and she looked up with a sinking feeling into John Tilton's face, only a few inches away. He was smiling at her with an odd mixture of tenderness and daring that made her suspect immediately that he had visited the Welsh cabin to enjoy that family's liquid version of Christmas cheer. The bandages were gone from his head, but an ugly new scar across his forehead was a reminder of his wounds. His injured leg was still tender, and a makeshift cane had become a part of his daily costume. But he was in full uniform—army blues and yellow kerchief knotted correctly at his neck inside the regulation overcoat. The clothes made him seem more formidable and threatening, as though he were ready again for action.

"I was thinking about home," she told him, hoping that he would not notice the few tears of homesickness that dampened her eyelashes.

However, if he noticed, it was satisfaction rather than sympathy he felt. "I said you would get tired of this place. Remember that?" He reached out and absently fingered one of the long curls that lay loosely on her shoulder, then let his fingers stray to the soft curve of her cheek. "The offer still stands, you know—bright lights, the city, beautiful gowns, and jewels. I can give you all that. We could go to San Francisco for a while and then maybe to Rio de Janeiro, even Paris, Vienna, Rome. Would you like that?"

Gloriana's fear did not cause her to fail to notice that he mentioned nothing of marriage. "You must be very rich," she faltered and tried to rise from the table where she had been working. But his right hand gripped her shoulder and held her in place while the left reached into his pocket. What he pulled from it at first stunned and then intrigued her—a heavy gold pendant with a large sea-green emerald set in a circle of pearls.

"A Christmas gift," he said and started to fasten it around her neck.

"Oh, but I cannot take it," Gloriana protested. "It's much too expensive!"

"It's nothing. As you said, I am very rich." Then he kissed her—fully on the lips, his mouth lingering on hers with a possessiveness and passion that repelled her as much as the sour smell of liquor on his breath. "We are good together, Gloriana," he breathed after a moment. "Norton is a fool to throw you over for a saloon keeper's daughter."

A few minutes later Gloriana burst into her uncle's office at the far end of the hospital to find him sitting with Graham Norton. It had not occurred to her that her uncle might be occupied, but she steeled herself to face Graham, remembering that he after all had been the one who asked her to watch John Tilton. When she told her story and showed them the emerald pendant, both men looked solemn, but it was Graham who asked the questions.

"He said he was rich and would take you to Paris and Vienna?" The blue eyes were cold and seemed to cut right through her. Otherwise his face was expressionless, the chiseled bronze mask of a stranger.

Gloriana nodded. "That struck me as strange," she explained, "because a soldier might be reassigned to Washington or even New York or New Orleans, but not to those places."

"Did he ask you to marry him?" Graham's voice was indifferent, and he did not look at her when he asked the question, but Gloriana was aware of the embarrassed flush that dyed her cheeks and the shake of her head that answered his question.

"I'm wondering where he got such an expensive jewel out here in the wilderness," Dr. Windemere interposed, fingering the bright pendant Gloriana had given him.

"Could it be a family heirloom?" Gloriana wondered.

"He wouldn't have it here," her uncle dismissed that idea. "If he is really as rich as he says, he would have his heirlooms in a bank back East, not here in his pocket. Besides, I'm not convinced by that story. Rich men are not usually army lieutenants!"

"You warned me about John Tilton months ago." Gloriana turned to Graham with a challenge in her eyes. She half suspected that he was holding something back—some key piece in the puzzle that he did not trust them, especially her, to be able to deal with. Besides, she could not let him think that just being near him made her tongue-tied and shy like a sixteen-year-old. "Now I want to know why."

Then it was Graham's turn for embarrassment. He shifted his position in the straight-backed chair, but he met her eyes when he responded. "I heard about him in Eureka after his troops had been bivouacked there. They said he couldn't be trusted with women and that his men roughed up some of the townspeople."

Outside, the sky was overcast again. Looking at the white denseness of clouds, Gloriana hoped that they were not in for one of the blizzards she had heard so much about. She had left her uncle's office with every intention of going to the Windemere cabin, but she found her feet turning toward the new chapel instead. She had carols to practice for the Christmas service, and somehow the thought of being at home where John Tilton might find her alone again sent a little shiver of dread down her spine.

A few minutes after she had left the hospital, she recognized, as surely as if she could see Graham Norton, the firm stride and the presence behind her.

When he caught up with her, they walked along in silence for several strides.

"I don't like the idea of your spending so much time with him," Graham said gruffly, staring straight ahead, his chin drawn into the turned-up collar of his jacket and his gloved hands stuffed into his pockets.

"I thought you wanted me to keep an eye on him," Gloriana retorted. The idea of the man—still wanting to run her life when he had taken himself so thoroughly out of it! Before she had really thought, she blurted out, "Well, it won't be for long now. I'll be going home in the spring, and then you can deal with Lieutenant Tilton on your own!"

"Have you really made up your mind?" He sounded startled, almost unbelieving.

"I have." She had not actually thought about it before, but it seemed like a good idea. Moreover, the statement had so shaken Graham out of his indifference that he looked almost hurt, before becoming suddenly, lividly angry.

"Gloriana Windemere, I knew you were an obstinate, prideful woman, but I never thought you were a coward." And he left her standing on the steps of the chapel. Had she gone too far? Or had she really meant what she had said?

Perhaps the only thing for me to do now is to go back home, Gloriana thought with a little sigh. Life had never been so complicated in Philadelphia. She could go back home and marry one of her father's young assistants—all serious, scholarly men who considered her background and skills qualifications for the perfect minister's wife. Or perhaps she would marry one of the doctors; most were too poor to afford a nurse and a wife both. She would be a bargain for one of them. The possibilities did not exactly thrill her, but that was to be expected.

Inside the chapel a crew of workmen hurried to finish, in time for Christmas services, the benches that would serve as pews. A new floor had been put in since Thanksgiving, and the walls had been plastered and whitewashed. Soldiers were there as well, sent by John Tilton to help with the finishing and decorating. Surprisingly the men were working together. They were not exactly friendly, but at least a truce of sorts seemed to have been called.

The blessed day brings peace, even here in the wilderness, Gloriana thought with a brief prayer for her own peace of mind.

Bridgette, her brothers, and some of the Klamath girls were decking the walls with evergreen garlands. From the girls' angry blushes and the boys' mischievous grins, Gloriana guessed that the Welsh males had been putting the mistletoe, which seemed in abundant supply, to good use.

"Miss Windemere, you are just in time to advise us on decorating the platform," Bridgette called out gaily. Two large fir trees stood in the choir loft already, their wide branches extending at one point to the organ bench.

"Why don't you just trim the trees?" Gloriana suggested without much enthusiasm. She did not relish the thought of playing the organ with an evergreen bough sticking in her back.

"How I wish we had tinsel and glass ornaments!" Bridgette was chattering on. "And wouldn't it be wonderful to have a Christmas ball? I told Graham that we would just have to have a ball when we are married in the spring, and you will be one of the first to receive an invitation, Miss Windemere."

Klamath Mission   New Year's Day, 1852

The new year is only hours old, and already it has brought sorrow. Catherine Midfield's baby was born prematurely last night, a tiny girl with dainty features like her mother and long, slim fingers. She only lived a few hours, and her parents' heartbreak is painful to witness. Dr. Midfield blames himself for trying to stay here when he knew his wife is delicate and likely to have a hard time.

I think she blames him too. There was anger as well as sorrow in her eyes when she was told about little Glorietta. They named her for me, and I too feel like a part of myself is gone with that baby, for I held her when she died, and not all my prayers could hold her here.

Uncle says that this is one of the times when we must simply trust and keep going. In my heart I know he is right, but my head keeps trying to understand how this could happen. Why should missionaries, good people like the Midfields, be called on for such a sacrifice? I know that in a modern hospital in the East Glorietta might have lived; perhaps there too Catherine would not have been under so much strain, and the baby would have gone to full term.

Possibly having Keintepoos in the house contributed to this tragedy, but somehow I think it would have happened anyway. In any case, the chief has been gone for more than a week. All we know is that he slipped away in a snowstorm with supplies from the hospital kitchen and his side half healed. Uncle has hopes that he has gone into hiding somewhere to wait out the winter. But I cannot help feeling that he left so that the mission would not be in danger. He did not expect to live when he came here, but as weeks went by and he realized the possible consequences to us of harboring a fugitive, he became desperate to escape. I could see it in his eyes.

Oweena fears he is dead. I have seen her watching the hills with tears in her eyes. Her anger against the soldiers grows almost daily, and I fear that she will say or do something that will place her life in even greater jeopardy than it already is.

And so the new year began in Oregon Territory. Time seemed suspended as blizzards roared down off the high plains and temperatures dropped to forty below. Several times it was necessary for parties of men to don snowshoes and forage for wood for the fires or food for people and animals. They ran out of coffee and sugar, and Dr. Windemere's pipe was once again empty. Yet the supply of spirits in the Welsh cabin seemed limitless, and during the long winter days with little to do and numbing cold to combat, more and more men—Indian and white alike—found their way to the trader's table.

Dr. Windemere had warned Mr. Welsh several times that a mission was no place for him to sell his wares. Each time the man had vigorously denied he was selling anything, but the traffic continued in and out of his cabin with a regularity that argued something more than social visits.

And not all Welsh's visitors made it home again. A miner whose claim was near Mount McLoughlin missed his way and walked off a bluff into Klamath Lake to resurface near the mission a few days later, his much-boasted pouch of nuggets gone from his pack. A trapper on his way south with a rich load of furs was found frozen to death on the lakeshore, and drifting snow revealed more than one unknown victim on the Umpqua Trail—the only passable route through the mountains.

Accidents? Perhaps. But the missionaries found themselves glancing over their shoulders when they went outside at night and even welcoming the presence of the soldiers as protection against an unknown menace.

"The Klamaths would never hurt us," Gloriana maintained stoutly, but she sensed a new fear in the Midfields, and even her uncle admitted he could not entirely forget the experience of the Whitmans and the Cayuse tribe.

"We lost many in the epidemic, and then gave shelter to the hated bluecoats," he reminded Gloriana.

A brooding danger, as gray and dark as the winter storms, seemed to have descended on the little mission, depressing the spirits of its inhabitants and infusing every wind with a menacing war cry.

If she could not feel safe outside, at least inside the Windemere cabin Gloriana found some relief.

Lieutenant Tilton had moved out at last to bunk

161

with his men and, Gloriana suspected, to join the nightly festivities at the trader's cabin. Still he did not forget her and holding him at arm's length was becoming more and more difficult. He had nicknamed her his "Puritan Maid" and seemed to accept their relationship as an established fact, but rarely did he mention his plans for them unless the boldness of drink was upon him. Then Gloriana feared him— enough that she carried in her pocket a small knife her brother had given her when she came west; and enough that, when she was alone at night, she watched the shadows for more than the mysterious raiders.

With the lieutenant gone Graham Norton resumed his nightly visits to the Windemere cabin. While the wind howled and the fire roared, he and the doctor would sit and finger their empty pipes and talk. Only now it was the Bible, not philosophy, that they discussed as Graham remembered the teachings of his childhood and sought to expand his understanding of the Christian walk.

Gloriana wondered how, as a Christian, he could plan to marry someone like Bridgette Welsh. She listened for news of their wedding from her uncle or Tildy or Dr. Midfield, with whom Graham had struck up a strong friendship. But with Graham himself she rarely exchanged a word. It was as though an impenetrable wall had been thrown up between them. Gloriana, had she but known it, assumed in his presence an icy hauteur that would have done justice to a Philadelphia matron, while Graham's cold indifference was a match.

Meanwhile the work of the mission crept along. Morning chapel services were better attended than usual—mostly, Dr. Windemere claimed, because there was nothing else to do. However, no new converts joined the fold. Business at the hospital was brisk with frostbite and victims of the mysterious attacks added to the usual list of ailments for treatment. And babies continued to be born, with Gloriana and Oweena as permanent nursemaids.

But overall little else happened. An atmosphere of waiting had descended over the mission. The lieutenant watched Gloriana and Oweena with unspoken plans in his dark eyes, but he could do nothing until spring. The soldiers and the Klamaths watched each other suspiciously, but both knew that any campaigns or battles would also wait until spring. Catherine Midfield's unhappiness was like a heavy weight that she carried with her, waiting for the spring. In the spring too Bridgette had said she would marry Graham Norton, and then Gloriana would have to make her own decision. Should she stay in Oregon Territory, or should she go back home to Philadelphia? Never, perhaps, had a spring been more fervently wished for and so justifiably feared.

CHAPTER 17

THE FIRST SIGNS OF WARMER WEATHER came from the ground rather than from the sky. March's thick, gray clouds still blotted out the sun, and sharp north winds still froze the shallow marshes around the edge of the Upper Klamath while they whipped the waters at lake center into icy, white-topped waves. Snow flurries continued at regular intervals to transform the drab landscape into a dazzling white wonderland. Yet underneath the snow pack the thaw had already begun. Unwary pedestrians, deviating from the shoveled mission pathways, found themselves breaking through a firm-looking crust into slush and cold water beneath. Soon the air was filled with the gurgling and trickling sounds of hundreds of tiny creeks, rushing under the melting snow or breaking through to tumble in icy sheets down the hillsides.

By the first of April most of the snow cover was gone. Wood violets began to appear in sheltered places in the forests, and buds formed on the pussy willows around the lake. The air was filled with the honking of northward bound flocks of geese while vividly colored wood ducks invaded the mission grounds in search of a handout.

The first of the mission's winter inhabitants to leave were Graham Norton and his men. His mule-drawn wagons rolled south toward Lost River country where they would begin blazing the Applegate Trail, a new freighting road that would eventually connect northern California with the Umpqua Valley in Oregon. Behind him Graham left the completed mission buildings—a new chapel with a bell tower, an orphanage with room for seventy children, a recreation hall that could double as a gymnasium, and an office-laboratory building large enough for all Dr. Windemere's records, as well as his lab equipment and experiments.

Graham also left a letter for Gloriana. Written in a clean, bold hand, its character was like that of the man—aggressive, to the point, and as mysterious as the green Oregon forests.

Dear Gloriana,

I can't leave without a final word, but since you and I can't seem to talk without fighting, I will write instead of saying it.

Whatever we might have meant to each other, I will always remember you as the one who showed me the way back to God. I could never talk about my parents' deaths. Suffice it to say that what I held against God then, I have now learned to accept, and I look forward to seeing my parents in heaven.

I hope you change your mind about going back to Philadelphia. We need you here, and if you will be honest with yourself, I think you will find that you need us too.

If you ever decide that you need me—well, we'll leave it in God's hands.

Graham

In her tiny room above the kitchen, Gloriana read the letter, wept over it, and prayed over it. Was it a goodbye? She tried to read an appeal for reconciliation into that final sentence or at least a door left open for the future, but there were too many unanswered questions. Did he still care for her, or was he merely grateful? If she needed him—was he offering help as a friend or as a lover? And what about Bridgette? What about the spring wedding? What about that kiss in the shadow of the organ the day before Thanksgiving?

Memories that had lain dormant during the winter, buried deep in her numbed heart, flooded back again, soft and bittersweet in the pale light of spring. Graham's voice, his touch, the way his red-gold hair curled on the back of his neck, the way his blue eyes warmed with laughter or his lips curved in a half smile—pictures haunted her dreams, waking or sleeping.

That she loved Graham, she could no longer deny. Her dreams betrayed her, overriding the stubborn denials of pride. In the fall when the glamor of romance was fresh and spellbinding, she had been overwhelmed by him and by the sensation of falling in love; her emotions had been close to the surface, rising and falling with the slightest provocation. Now her feelings seemed more deeply rooted—more at the center of her being and less separable from the fabric of her personality. The man had somehow ceased to be an external and had become an internal force in her life.

This must be what they call "true love," Gloriana realized with a mixture of awe and despair. That she could care so deeply for someone who had betrayed her seemed incredible. Yet as surely as she recognized that her feelings could exist independently, regardless of her conscious wishes, Gloriana knew that nothing could or would change them. She could go back home to Philadelphia, Graham could marry Bridgette, she could see him every day or never again, but she knew that she would go on loving this man as long as she lived.

Oddly enough, accepting the fact brought her a kind of peace. There was no longer a need to struggle. The matter was out of her control—in "the Lord's hands," as Graham had said, and if Gloriana could not quite bring herself to believe in the man she loved, she knew she could trust her Heavenly Father.

Klamath Mission   April 15, 1851

Spring in Oregon Territory is a magic time. All the gloom and suffering of the fall and winter are far from forgotten, but it is possible to hope again.

We pray for peace! Yet the spring that promises so much brings also the threat of increased hostilities. A small Mormon community just fifteen miles to the west of us was burned to the ground a few nights ago. Klamath scouts brought us word of the massacre, but they would say nothing about who had done it.

Lieutenant Tilton and his soldiers continue at the mission, but I feel their presence here grows less and less friendly. Daily they scour the country on patrols, but it seems their movements are observed, for no sooner do they ride to the west, than the renegades attack in the east. Oweena is watched constantly while the lieutenant questions us all about Keintepoos. I fear that somehow he has learned the truth, and I remember all too well his threats.

"Gloriana, dear, I am afraid I left my spectacles on the pulpit in the chapel. I wonder if you would mind fetching them for your old uncle." Dr. Windemere appealed to her from his favorite armchair. A book rested in his lap; his feet, on a low footstool. From the way he moved Gloriana guessed that the arthritis she suspected was affecting his knees had intensified with the damp weather. "Just a touch of rheumatism," her uncle added, as though he had read her thoughts.

"It will only take me a minute," she said, and, grabbing up a hand-knitted shawl against the chill that still lingered in the spring breeze, she set out for the chapel.

The afternoon sun had dipped low over the lake,

167

paving a golden path across the surface. A circus of waterfowl was rising and settling in the tules, and the air echoed with its joyous sounds. Overhead the sky was a pastel blue with white misty clouds as trimmings. Underneath Gloriana's feet the ground felt moist and spongy. A light veil of new green was beginning to color the rolling, hummocky hills and make a bower of the willow grove around the artesian spring in the quadrangle.

Gloriana cut across the quadrangle by the little path that went past the spring. She heard the bubbling waters before she realized the sounds were mixed with angry voices, a man and a woman fighting. Not wanting to overhear something that was not meant for her ears, she started to turn back; then she realized that the voices belonged to Lieutenant Tilton and Bridgette Welsh and she paused, fascinated in spite of herself.

"You said we could leave here in the spring." Bridgette's tone was shrill and accusing. "You promised me San Francisco and beautiful gowns and jewels."

Gloriana suppressed a little gasp. That was exactly what John Tilton had promised *her!* What kind of game was he playing?

"You know, you're beginning to be tiresome," the man's voice responded, managing to sound both annoyed and bored. "I am starting to wonder what I ever saw in you."

"If you think you can just use me and then walk away, you had better think again. I know enough to ruin you. What would precious Gloriana Windemere say if she knew where you got your money? What if I told her who you really are?"

There was a sharp sound that could have been a slap, followed by a woman's crying. Gloriana knew she should run but she was frozen in place, stunned by what she was hearing.

"If you ever say a word to her, I will fix your face so no man will ever look at you again."

"John, please," Bridgette was pleading now, "you don't want her. We're good together. I can give you much more than she ever could."

"You already have," the man sneered. Gloriana could feel the cruelty without seeing his face. "You might take a lesson from Miss Windemere. Never give yourself to a man before the wedding. No man, not even that big oaf Norton, will want to marry a tramp."

Gloriana turned and ran back down the pathway, holding her skirts high to keep them from rustling or tripping her. The soft ground cushioned and absorbed the sound of her footfalls, but she held her breath, almost afraid to exhale for fear she might be heard.

She was astonished at what she had learned. Not the least of her amazement came from the realization that Bridgette Welsh was jealous of her. The beautiful minx, who had so skillfully maneuvered her way between Graham and Gloriana, secretly saw Gloriana as a rival. Gloriana could almost pity the girl. If what Tilton had implied about their relationship was true, Bridgette must have expected to win him with weapons Gloriana could not and would not use. But what about Graham? If Bridgette was planning to elope with Tilton, she must have abandoned her plan to marry Graham Norton. For a moment Gloriana's heart sang at the prospect. Yet what if Graham knew nothing of Bridgette's change of heart? Wouldn't she be all the more likely, now that she had been rejected by Tilton, to go through with her original plans?

Even more puzzling were Bridgette's hints about the lieutenant's money and some hidden identity. If only she could talk to Graham!

Something is wrong here, very wrong, Gloriana told herself as she navigated an alternate route to the chapel. Such an understatement might have made her smile if she had not been trembling so hard.

She found the doctor's spectacles on the pulpit, right where he had said he left them. The wire frames were slightly bent, and they sat at an angle on his nose, giving him a puzzled look as he listened to Gloriana's account of what she had overheard.

"Isn't it amazing how our own insecurities can give power to our enemies?" he commented when she told him about Bridgette's jealousy.

Gloriana did not have to ask what he meant. She knew. Because of her own feelings of insecurity—the sense that she was too old, not pretty enough, not appealing to men—she had let Bridgette Welsh come between her and Graham. She had not fought back but had just accepted her own defeat. Well, if she ever had a second chance, she would have enough faith in herself and in God to make the most of the opportunity.

For the rest, Dr. Windemere had little to say. Like Gloriana, he wished Graham Norton were there, but since Graham was not, he said, they would have to wait and see.

"Back home we would call the police, and they would check out what I heard," Gloriana wrote in her journal that evening. "Here we are alone—far from any official help. The nearest magistrate is at Applegate Landing, and the nearest fort, at Winnemucca, two hundred miles away, across lava flows, canyons, mountains, and desert.

Dear God, help us, Gloriana found herself breathing the prayer unconsciously.

Feeling alone and isolated, she was not prepared for a knock at the door. The firm rapping echoed through the cabin, sending a chill down her spine and making the breath catch in her throat.

"Don't be silly," she scolded herself. "It's probably Dr. Midfield to check on uncle's aching limbs." The young doctor had been especially sympathetic the past few days, taking over most of the older man's

170

duties and urging him to rest. Privately Gloriana suspected that her uncle's colleague was preparing to leave the mission and was feeling guilty about leaving the Windemeres to carry on alone.

But it was not Dr. Midfield at the cabin door. Lieutenant John Tilton leaned against the doorsill, a bouquet of wildflowers in his hand and a dazzling smile on his handsome face.

"If I had come to visit you at your home in Philadelphia," he told Gloriana, "I would have brought roses, but these are the best I can do here."

Gloriana stammered her thanks, but she did not invite him in. "Uncle has gone to bed early." As she started to make the excuse, he pushed past her with a grin that showed his delight at the prospect of being alone with her.

With the familiarity of a long-time house guest, he placed his hat on the rack behind the door and his gloves on the table beneath.

"I have a lot to tell you." Neither his voice nor expression revealed the villainy that had been so apparent in his conversation with Bridgette just a few hours before. It amazed Gloriana that he could look and smile so happily after such a scene, and she searched his face for some sign of remorse or embarrassment.

Instead he appeared eager; in other circumstances, Gloriana might have mistaken the warmth in his eyes for love. He drew her to the sofa with its vivid coverings of Indian blankets and sat so close to her that she could almost hear the stiff material of his uniform creak with the pressure of measured breaths.

"Miss Windemere—Gloriana—I have received a dispatch from Washington; I am being transferred. It means a promotion and new post back in civilization, and I want you to go with me—as my wife."

The proposal, when she had expected a proposition, was completely surprising. But she knew he was

171

lying. Only one letter had come for him in the mail pouch that had arrived from Applegate Landing a few days before. Gloriana had sorted the mail herself, and she remembered the distinctive stationery marked with the return address of a San Francisco hotel.

"This is so sudden," she began lamely.

But instead of being offended, he seemed to expect her conventionality and even to be pleased by it. "You must know I care for you," he said earnestly, and slipping down on one knee, he took her hand and pressed it to his lips.

Gloriana felt distant, as though she were watching such a romantic scene from outside herself. Irrelevantly, she remembered her objections when Graham had made his impulsive proposal in the open mission yard with dozens of eyes watching.

"Have you spoken with my uncle?" Not able to say what she really felt, it seemed safest to continue with the accepted formula.

"Only say the word, and I will speak to him."

Absently Gloriana wondered what this man—this devil in uniform, as she now thought of him—had in mind for her. Surely not an honorable marriage! Or perhaps he did intend to marry her. It was entirely possible, Gloriana realized, that he had interpreted the tinge of coldness she had not been able to keep from her manner to him as a sign of her being a very proper and cultured lady. Gloriana herself had known many society matrons and debutantes who equated coldness with refinement, and she knew enough of human nature to acknowledge the attractiveness a ladylike woman might have for a man as depraved as this one.

Yet when she searched his face for evidence of that depravity, she saw only a smooth, handsome face and dark, appealing eyes that glowed with an apparent affection for her. She could almost doubt that the conversation she had overheard that afternoon had taken place, but in her memory she could still hear the anguish in Bridgette's voice.

How easy it would be for a young woman to be taken in by this man, Gloriana told herself while she met his gaze, marveling in the ability of a foul nature to clothe itself in comeliness. And for the first time she truly felt sorry for Bridgette. Little more than a child and frantic to escape from the frontier, she must have seen Lieutenant Tilton as the answer to her prayers.

"I will need time to think," Gloriana remembered to murmur as she glanced down at the hand he held.

"But there is no time," he answered, pressing closer and moving as though to encircle her waist with his arm. Unable to stand it any longer, Gloriana stood up abruptly and suggested tea. Tilton looked startled but smiled as though she were merely being shy, and he dropped a sly kiss on her cheek as she dodged away.

Out in the kitchen Gloriana rubbed her cheek vigorously with her handkerchief and tried to overcome her intense physical revulsion. Never had she been more repelled, but she knew instinctively that she dared not show it. She wished she could call her uncle, but she also feared for his safety.

"If only Graham Norton were here," she thought for the hundredth time and regretted more than ever her pride—it had kept her from listening to him and had allowed him to believe that she could be interested in the dangerously fascinating John Tilton.

The water had been heated and tea brewed before she remembered that she had left her journal sitting on the table under the lamp. Praying that Tilton had not noticed it, she put the tea things on a tray and hurried back to the living room just in time to see the lieutenant slipping several torn pages into his pocket. If she had had any doubt about where the pages came from, the fury in the dark gaze he turned on her was enough to tell Gloriana he had read the journal.

173

"I find I cannot stay after all," he said smoothly. His voice still sounded pleasant, almost soothing, but his eyes glared dangerously. Gloriana was reminded of the beautiful Mount McLoughlin—a paradise on the outside but molten lava within.

She followed him, not knowing what to say, to the door.

"I think we can assume that I have your answer to my proposal." He must have read some of her comments about him. Gloriana caught her breath and tried to think of an explanation, some excuse to carry on the deception.

But the game was over. The man turned; his look, traveling insolently up and down her body, made her heart stop with terror.

"You must know that if I can't have you one way, I will have you another." And he smiled, the familiar dazzling smile, but with a touch of malice that made the expression menacing. Before Gloriana knew what was happening, he had seized her wrists and pinned them behind her back. His lips, bruising her cheeks and searing her neck, were harsh, and the embrace was a cruel punishment instead of a caress.

Then he was gone, leaving Gloriana shaking. She bathed her cheeks with cold water and poured herself a cup of the neglected tea with hands that could barely hold the pot steady.

Picking up the journal, she began to leaf through the pages to find what he had taken. All that was missing were the sketches she had made months ago—drawings of the renegade Shastas beside the creek on the Crescent City Trail.

CHAPTER 18

THE NEXT DAY the soldiers rode out. In a column of twos, they crossed the mission yard and headed along the lakeshore. Standing on the steps, Gloriana was too far away to make out the expressions on the men's faces, but she could feel the menace in the lieutenant's attitude and sense the mockery in his salute as he turned to wave at her.

"At least we will have nothing to fear from him for awhile," she told herself with relief. The soldiers had commandeered supplies from the mission stores, and their packs bulged with enough food for a long campaign. Gloriana prayed that wherever the army searched, Chief John and Keintepoos, if he were still alive, would be somewhere else. Her thoughts turned to the young chief and she remembered him as she had first seen him—strong and impassive but with a gleam of humor lurking in his dark, intelligent eyes. Somehow she doubted he were dead, and she believed it would take more than an arrogant lieutenant to capture him.

She felt almost lighthearted as she bathed the two

babies in the infant ward and fed a child whose burned hands were wrapped in bandages. The heavy wooden shutters over the windows had been opened, and the fresh smells of spring wafted through the open casements. Birds were singing ecstatically in the willows on the quadrangle. Sunbeams like liquid gold decorated the bare, scrubbed floor.

Into this happy morning burst Bridgette Welsh with a tear-stained face and fury that bordered on hysteria.

"It's your fault he's gone," Bridgette cried accusingly. She stumbled between the beds of curious patients to corner Gloriana in the dispensary. Pointing a finger at Gloriana and clenching her other hand into a fist, Bridgette looked as though she planned to strike her rival. But no blows came, only more angry words accompanied by such an explosion of fury and abuse that Gloriana felt slightly bewildered.

"I really don't know what you're talking about," she assured the distraught young woman.

"Don't give me your innocent act. He thinks you're pure because you're so cold. But I know better. I saw you kissing Graham Norton in the snow, and those were not the kisses of a shy, innocent girl.

"You think you're so much better than I. 'A lady of taste and intelligence,' John said, but you're not so smart. I took your precious Norton away from you by throwing myself into his arms and kissing him. And you—you are so dumb that you never even knew that he didn't kiss back."

If Bridgette had hoped to hurt Gloriana with her revelation, she could not have been wider of the mark.

"You even believed me when I said I was going to marry him," Bridgette spat out with a scornful little laugh. "Well, maybe I lost John Tilton because of you, but I fixed it so you can't have Graham Norton either. The way you have treated him all these months and the way you threw yourself at my John, you'll be lucky if Norton even speaks to you again."

But he had! When Bridgette had gone, in a flurry of flying skirts and a storm of sobs, Gloriana remembered Graham's farewell letter. Perhaps she had hurt him too badly with her jealousy. Perhaps his love had been killed and all he had left for her was friendship. Nevertheless, there was a chance, and Gloriana was glad that both of them had decided to leave their romance in the Lord's hands.

That's certainly a safer place than in my hands, Gloriana thought ruefully. What a mess she had made of things! Her uncle had suggested her insecurity was at fault; she thought now it was more likely her vanity. She had expected Graham to ignore that girl as though she didn't exist, and then at the first opportunity sent him straight into her arms. She remembered the day of her engagement. *Why didn't I go with him, as he asked me?* Bridgette had been all over him; he must have been trying to get away from her without ceasing to act like a gentleman. Pride had dictated her actions then, and pride would have destroyed her future if it had not been for Bridgette's angry outburst.

"For we know that all things work together for good to them that love the Lord, to them who are called according to His purpose." She recalled the Scripture with a feeling of awe.

The Welsh family left the next day, their still heavily loaded wagons rolling north across the open grasslands to the site of their new trading post. A few of the younger men from the Klamath village went with them, Welsh said, as guides, but Dr. Windemere disagreed. "I fear they are following rather than leading, and the attraction is Welsh's firewater, as the Indians call it."

With the departure of the Welshes, the raids on nearby settlers and lone trappers and miners also seemed to stop. Could Welsh have been the instigator? Could he have used his liquor to make the young

177

Klamaths kill for him? The missionaries discussed the matter with each other and then with the mission Indians. There was no way to reach a conclusion, but the suspects' being miles away made the little community feel more comfortable, if no less concerned.

"Remind me never to allow a settlement to grow up here," Dr. Windemere told Gloriana as he watched children playing in the mission yard from his cabin porch. The mail carrier from Applegate Landing had brought him a fresh supply of tobacco and, with his pipe in one hand and a book in the other and his swollen knees elevated on a stool, he was content.

Thankfully the spring had so far brought no outbreak of measles, influenza, typhoid, or diphtheria—the special demons of frontier communities and killers of whites as well as Indians. In fact, the warm afternoons had nearly emptied the hospital, and Gloriana and Oweena took long rambles along the lake.

Still, Gloriana did not forget about John Tilton. She feared that they had not seen the last of him, and whenever she picked up her journal, she was puzzled about the missing pages. Why would he want her drawings of those renegades? Perhaps he planned to use them to identify the real killers. Yet why would that make him so angry?

They were questions without answers, and they hung there, in the back of Gloriana's mind, infusing the perfect days with a faint uneasiness, a vague anxiety that made her glance fearfully over her shoulder in the twilight or jump at the sound of a knock on the door.

Nearly two weeks to the day after the soldiers left the mission, Gloriana awoke at dawn. An unnatural quiet, like the hush in the eye of the storm, had jarred her from a nightmarish sleep in which she had been running blindly from some unnamed fear. The eastern

178

sky was dimly lit, but no morning chorus of bird songs came from the willow grove. No meadowlarks greeted the dawn from their grassy hiding places, and on the lake the ducks and geese were strangely silent.

Slipping on a robe, Gloriana opened the wooden shutters of her window and peered out. Nothing moved in the mission yard—no dog, no early-rising child, no hunter, no squaw going for water at the artesian spring. Then below her in the shadow of the cabin, she saw the small yellow flame of a match, and she knew her uncle also had been awakened by the stillness.

"They're all gone," he told her when Gloriana joined him below. "There's no one in the cabins or the hospital. I walked over to the village, and everyone has left." The doctor did not look frightened, merely very old and very tired.

"What does it mean?" Gloriana asked with a little shiver that was less the result of the morning chill than of the eeriness of the moment.

"They were afraid. There's fear in the air. Even the birds feel it and are quiet and hiding." While he was talking, Tildy hurried out of the adjoining cabin to say that her girls were gone. Dr. Midfield and Catherine came running from the hospital to tell them what they already knew: the patients were gone. No horses remained in the mission corral nor any milk cows in the barn. Not so much as a bantam chicken remained in its coop, nor a rabbit in its hutch.

"This awful Oregon!" Catherine cried, burying her face with a little sob in her husband's shoulder.

Looking from one to another, the missionaries knew that they were all thinking about the same thing—a silent morning on the Walla Walla River broken by a shrill cry and the slaughter of the Whitmans and twelve members of their household.

"These people are our friends. They would never harm us!" Gloriana protested against the unspoken terror she saw reflected from face to face.

179

"This is a risk we took," Dr. Windemere had started to comment resignedly when they heard pounding hoofs across the grasslands. Echoes from the hills multiplied the sound so that the missionaries, steeling themselves for an attack, were startled to see a single Indian pony round the chapel and cut across the mission yard.

At first there appeared to be no rider; then they saw a small figure, that had been nearly covered by the flying mane, leap from the pony's back and run to embrace Gloriana. It was Oweena.

"I saw him. He's coming for you," she cried, the words tumbling over each other. "My people thought they were the ones he wanted; they thought you would be safe. But I've seen him and I know. You must get away; use the tules as cover until you're in the forest. I go for help." She did not seem to hear their questions but leaped back on the pony's back and was gone.

"Gloriana, what was she talking about? Who could be after you?" Catherine Midfield demanded.

"Could it be Chief John?" Tildy suggested.

Gloriana could not answer, though she felt somehow that she should know; her brain was numb with the horror of the situation.

"We must all go," she began confusedly, looking around as though she expected to find some means of escape near at hand. The sun was rising, sending a soft, rosy glow over the mission; it did not look like a scene for violence, yet the emptiness was like an ominous, waiting presence.

Dr. Windemere relit his pipe slowly. "My place is here with my work," he said finally.

To Gloriana's amazement the others agreed. "It makes no sense to just stay here and wait," she protested, but their minds were made up.

"How can we escape?" Dr. Midfield asked. "The horses are gone. We have no idea in which direction to go."

"Oweena said she would bring help," Tildy reminded them all.

They joined hands for a moment of prayer, and Dr. Windemere's steady voice betrayed no anxiety. "Our Heavenly Father, we trust You on this day as on every other to watch over us. Keep us in Your will whatever the storms of life may bring. Give us the strength for each trial we must face and the grace to accept what we cannot change. Give us the courage to do Your work during the night as well as the day, and give us the peace of knowing that You are the Friend who will stay closer than a brother, that when all others forsake us, You will still be there." He finished, and the quiet strength in the old doctor's prayer inspired a confidence in his staff that calmed, if not completely extinguished, their fears. "We may be close to home this morning," he added with a look of genuine affection for each of them. "I for one would not object too greatly to taking my supper with the Master. Now let's all get dressed and see about breakfast."

This attitude of simple acceptance was a revelation to Gloriana. She admired it and recognized it as an integral part of the missionary spirit. They had all known the dangers when they answered the call to the Oregon Territory, and they would face those dangers as uncomplainingly as they faced the hard work and the loneliness of frontier life.

For herself, waiting was not the answer. Oweena had suggested action, and Gloriana was beginning to conceive a plan. Somewhere to the south at a place called Lost River, Graham Norton and his men were building a road. She would find them and bring them back.

In the bottom of her trunk she found a riding habit—wrinkled and unfamiliar, yet sturdy and comfortable enough for travel. She had never been much of a horsewoman, but her sisters had insisted the garments were necessary to a Western wardrobe. Silently blessing them for the forethought, she slipped into the split skirt and heavy blouse and found a jacket that would protect her against thorns and branches as well as against the cold. She had boots and long, knitted socks as well as a knapsack. As an after-thought she added a broad-brimmed hat and long leather gloves and stuffed her journal and Bible and a lighter weight blouse into the knapsack.

Tildy was not yet in the kitchen, so there was no one to question her as she added biscuits and cheese to the knapsack. If they knew what she intended, they would never let her go, no matter how urgent Oweena's warning had been; therefore, Gloriana moved cautiously through the door.

The road to the forest, a two-wheel rut through the turf, was the shorter way; ahead tall timber began abruptly where the lakeshore rose in razor-back hills. The trees were spaced closely together, the gaps between Ponderosas and firs closed by dense growths of manzanita and jack pines. The forest looked safe, and invitingly secret, but after a moment's hesitation Gloriana headed for the thick stands of brush and tules along the lake's edge instead. *It will be slower, but I won't have to cross any open space this way*, she thought, recalling Oweena's warning to move under cover.

Behind her the mission buildings appeared solid and peaceful in the clear morning light. *Oweena said they—whoever "they" are—are after me. Perhaps the others will be safe with me gone*. She had no definite idea where Lost River might be. She only knew that it was somewhere to the south.

The tules and bushes fringing Klamath Lake formed a shoulder-high screen and by bending over, she could make good time without being seen from either the mission or the forest. To her surprise the undergrowth was not deserted; ducks and even some of the mission chickens and rabbits hid in the rushes and under the banks. They darted from one cover to the next as she ran by, but they did not make a sound, and the birds did not fly away.

The ground along the shore was soft and spongy in places, but slippery with sand in others. Several times she stumbled, and the gritty, miry coating that soon covered her gloves made her glad she had remembered to wear them.

Gradually as she neared the forest, a feeling grew that some unseen presence watched and waited there. Almost without realizing she was doing so, Gloriana slowed her pace and ducked down until she was crawling instead of running, and she moved carefully to avoid making a sound.

She wondered if this presence were what the animals felt—a dark, brooding menace on the edge of consciousness, like a sudden movement seen from the corner of the eye or a noise half heard in the night. And she was moving toward it rather than away from it. Every nerve told her to turn and run, but a small inner voice kept urging her toward rather than away from the shadows.

"The Lord is my Shepherd . . . Yea, though I walk through the valley of the shadow of death, I will fear no evil; for thou art with me; thy rod and thy staff, they comfort me." Never had she felt more like a lost sheep and never had she prayed harder for the crook of the Shepherd's staff to close around her and lift her from the precipice where she had wandered.

At the edge of the lake where the grasslands gave way to mountains and trees, two forest giants had fallen. Their branches, now bare of green, were intertwined, and their roots had torn a shallow cave in the brush and turf. Creeping thankfully into the shelter, Gloriana tried to catch her breath. Her side ached and the air entered her lungs with sharp stabs.

A veil of grasses, soap brush, and manzanita

shielded the entrance to the cave, but through that green curtain Gloriana could see past the eaves into the dark aisles of the forest. She had watched, unseeing, for several minutes before she became aware of moving shadows amid the tree trunks. A moment later she recognized the flowing hair and sashed shirts of the renegades.

Like a nightmare her mind flashed back to a cool stream on a hot day, and she heard again Graham Norton's command to look over her shoulder. The menacing faces on the other side of the water came back in vivid detail, and even as she watched him stalk from the cover of a giant fir tree, Gloriana realized that she knew the leader of this war party.

CHAPTER 19

SUDDENLY THE PIECES OF THE PUZZLE began to fit together—the strange lawlessness of himself and his men, the warnings, the feeling they had met before, the sketches torn from her journal, the promises of riches and escape. For the leader of these so-called renegades was none other than John Tilton—savage and fierce looking in his costume and war paint but still clearly recognizable in the morning light.

He thought I recognized him when I made those drawings! Gloriana thought, as stunned by the fact she had not as by the killer's identity.

Her first impulse was to return to the mission and warn the others, but she knew it was too late. "It's me he wants," she whispered, realizing the truth of Oweena's strange warning and, with a shiver, the necessity for her own escape.

It seemed like hours since she had left the cabin, but the sun, still low on the eastern horizon, told her that no more than a few minutes had passed. Leaving this cover would be impossible until Tilton's men had left the forest, and then she would have to move fast before they discovered she was not at the mission and began to hunt for her.

Revolted by the thought of food but knowing she needed strength, Gloriana took some jerked meat from her knapsack and tried to eat, but the food stuck in her throat when she tried to swallow.

The outlaws seemed to be waiting for something. They moved about or crouched under the trees, but mostly they watched. From somewhere back in the trees came the sound of horses' stamping and blowing.

Gloriana wondered how long their Indian friends had known of the identity of the so-called renegades; she suspected at least since Keintepoos's injury. Probably the missionaries' helping the soldiers—undoubtedly the aggressors rather than the victims, as they claimed, of the battle with the Klamath chiefs—had created an atmosphere of distrust. Or perhaps the Indians, including Oweena, felt that the missionaries, being white themselves, would not believe an accusation made against white men.

The cave was warm, but Gloriana did not remove her jacket. She would have to be ready to move at any moment, and she could not risk leaving it behind. Another hour passed. She woke from a light doze to see Tilton pointing toward the grasslands; her eyes followed to see puffs of smoke rising from the opposite shore of the lake.

They don't know the Mission is almost deserted and are attacking from both sides. She breathed a prayer of thanks that the villagers and the children were gone and at the same time saw the wisdom of Oweena's advice. Going toward the forest she had met one band of outlaws, but in the other direction she would soon have run out of cover and been captured.

Dear God, help them, Gloriana breathed a prayer for the mission staff as Tilton gave the signal to advance. Tears filled her eyes, but she hoisted her pack and prepared to move.

The outlaws were attacking on foot, leaving their horses behind in the trees. There would be a guard, but perhaps there would be a way to get one of the horses.

Gloriana's heart was pounding, and her knees were shaking again as she slipped from the shelter of the fallen trees and crawled in the direction of the restless animals. A stand of firs screened her movements while thick mats of pine needles cushioned and muffled her steps.

The horses were held in a grassy hollow and, to Gloriana's relief, she saw they had been hobbled rather than tethered. Some of the more adventurous had already drifted from the herd, tempted by greener grass down the next aisle of trees or in the next glade. Tilton was apparently not expecting any trouble, for he had posted only one guard—a sleepy-looking young man whom Gloriana thought she recognized, even in his long-haired wig and paint, as the trooper they called Lazy Harry. He was not watching the horses but was whittling idly with his pocket knife on a piece of wood. He looked bored, and Gloriana wondered with a little shudder how many other times he had watched like this.

Except for the occasional whinny of a horse or the sharp crack of a shod hoof against a tree trunk, the forest was still. The usual scolding of the squirrels and the chattering of the jays were ominously absent, while no scurryings in the underbrush signaled the woodland folk's hurrying about their day's business.

One horse, the boldest of all, had climbed out of the hollow and was hobbling determinedly toward a lush patch of grass in the sun. Gloriana, hidden beneath the drooping branches of a blue spruce, watched the guard for any sign of concern, but he did not so much as glance in the animal's direction. Then, being careful to keep heavy cover between herself and the inquisitive horse, Gloriana followed.

It was John Tilton's own saddle mount, a large, powerful roan with an intelligent eye and a body built for both speed and endurance. He apparently recognized Gloriana, for he did no more than shy away as she tried to approach him.

"Here, Champion," Gloriana called, remembering the great beast's name. His long ears flicked back and forth, listening to the sound of her voice. "Always talk softly to horses," Gloriana recalled Oweena saying. "They are nervous animals, and your voice will soothe them." She tried whispering but Champion jerked away at the sound and she changed to a soft murmur, hoping the sound would not carry to the waiting guard. "Such a pretty horse. Nice Champion. Big, strong Champion."

Her repeated use of his name reassured the intelligent beast. He went on cropping the tender spring grass while she put her fingertips on his velvety nose and rubbed gently between his ears. Then she had her hands on the reins and was leading him to a fallen tree trunk where she could mount.

Fervently wishing she were a better horsewoman, Gloriana struggled to remove the hobbles and then struggled again to get into the saddle. Champion turned and looked at her inquiringly over his shoulder, as though puzzled by her difficulties. But he did not buck and after a few crabsteps, resisting the strange touch on the reins, he began to settle down and accept her directions. "You probably think I am taking you to your master," she resumed talking to the high-strung animal, "but I'm not. You see, we have had a kind of falling out, and I am going to have to take you far away. You'll like it where we are going, though. There will be warm stalls and lots of hay and oats to eat someday in Applegate Landing. But first we have to take a little trip south to a place called Lost River. I'm not exactly sure where it is, but I know we can find it if we just try hard enough."

Champion's ears were turned toward her, and gradually she felt the jumpiness leave his big body and his teeth quit searching for the bit in his mouth. Gloriana had never ridden such a large, powerful horse before. She rarely managed to be completely in charge of any mount, and this one could easily run away with her or rub her off his back on the nearest low-hanging branch. But Champion was well trained and, if not exactly eager to please, he was at least willing.

"I guess the Shepherd's staff found me once again," Gloriana realized with a prayer of thankfulness. On foot it would only have been a matter of time before they found her, but astride this magnificent animal, she had a chance—at least she would have a chance if she figured out which direction to go in.

Although she had lived on the nearby Upper Klamath for eight months or more, she had never been this far into the woods before. The sameness of the trees, the bushy undergrowth, the sudden hills, and equally sudden ravines was bewildering. Overhead, interlocking branches blotted out the sun, creating a green twilight, and it was difficult to tell whether a distant rushing sound was from the soughing of a breeze in the treetops or the tumbling waters of a nearby stream.

Every impulse told Gloriana to bury herself in the forest. Hidden in this maze of trees, she would feel safe from pursuit. Yet she had heard about travelers, lost in the forest, who moved in circles for hours, never going far from their starting point. She thought about giving Champion his head and letting him find his way south. In fact, if left to his devices, he would probably rejoin the other horses, and, unable to tell north from south, she might not even know they had changed direction until it was too late.

"I will instruct thee and teach thee in the way in

which thou should go. I will guide thee with mine eyes," she remembered the promises and set out another urgent appeal for guidance.

It was then that she remembered that Klamath Lake ran directly north and south. If she could find the lakeshore, she could follow it south, staying within the protecting shadows of wooded hills the entire way.

Finding the lake turned out to be an easy enough matter. The hills sloped down to the shore all along the west side and by continually following the downward slopes, she soon saw pale blue waves gleaming in the sunshine.

Almost at the same time she became aware of the faint sounds of a battle. Carried across the waters were gunshots and what sounded like distant war cries, but peering almost into the sun, she could see nothing. *Protect them, God,* she prayed again and again. She wondered what was happening. Who was fighting? The missionaries would not be; their way, like that of the martyrs, was a passive acceptance which in itself condemned the violence. Perhaps Oweena had returned with help as she promised. Perhaps the phony warriors of the murderer Tilton were now engaged in battle with real warriors. Gloriana had no way of knowing, and with tears in her eyes, she turned Champion's head south and urged him to a gallop.

Bordering the fresh-water lake, the forest grew taller and lusher. Instead of the scrub pines, thick firs, and rocky, brush-covered soil of the hillsides, giant Ponderosas were separated by wide, cool aisles nearly free of undergrowth. Champion moved tirelessly through this dim, green world. His galloping hooves startled an occasional deer from its cover or sent birds winging through the branches. Yet the farther south they went, the more alive the forest became. Saucy jays or camp robbers mocked them from the treetops, then followed for a short distance on dark blue wings, as though, having given them an ultimatum, they were making sure the intruders left their domain. The bushes rustled with unseen inhabitants as the horse and rider passed, and once a silver fox darted across the trail. How could the wildlife know the awful portent of a war party and go into hiding, yet accept the intrusion of a lone woman as little more than a temporary annoyance? It could be the numbers. At least thirty men had been in John Tilton's party. Or it could be a sixth sense, a built-in warning which made the animals aware of the evil purposes of the men. Gloriana remembered the dark presence that she had felt and guessed the latter.

She sensed no such presence following her now. Often her head turned automatically to look for pursuers, but no one was visible, and she felt no one behind her. Gradually she became aware of a difficulty in breathing and a sharp stitch in her side that increased with each jarring motion of the big roan's haunches. The pain subsided a little if she held him to a walk or increased his pace to a run, but it returned as soon as Champion resumed the gallop.

"You are holding up magnificently," she told him finally, "but I am afraid I am going to have to rest." The bank of a small stream offered green grass for the horse to eat and a soft couch for Gloriana to sit on. She eased herself gingerly from the saddle, trying not to notice the charley horses in each thigh or the soreness of her backside.

Although she had brought food, she had forgotten a canteen, and the clear water of the stream, icy with the continued run-off of melting snow at some high elevation, soothed her face and cooled her parched throat. She noticed how the animal did not drink his fill but took a few mouthfuls and then moved away to graze and wait for his warm flanks to cool before drinking deeply. Remembering that too much ice-cold water when a patient is warm can cause stomach cramps, Gloriana followed suit, and soon she was feeling more comfortable.

The irony of her escaping on John Tilton's horse made her want to laugh, though the ache in her side from the unaccustomed hours on Champion prevented more than a smile. But even the smile disappeared as she looked through the trees to see billowing smoke rising from the direction of the mission on the other side of the lake. *Dear God, they're burning it!* She thought of the beautiful new chapel, the orphanage, the snug cabins. Before she had felt only fear; now a fierce anger began to grow inside her. "He won't get away with this, and this time he will suffer the consequences."

With riding and resting it took nearly seven hours to skirt the giant lake. The sun was halfway to the western horizon when Champion stepped from the protecting forest onto the sands of the Klamath's south shore, and Gloriana realized that from here she would have to find her way by instinct.

"I wish you could talk," she told the horse once again. "I have a feeling your instincts would be more reliable than mine in this situation."

The sun, beginning its western descent, was on her right. Before her was open range—rolling grasslands, wooded shelves, and shadowed valleys, stretching away to deserts in the south and east and more mountains in the west. Crisscrossing that vast gray-green space were meandering bands of dark green, each one of which might be the one they called the Lost River.

Why would they call a river "lost"? How could anyone lose a river? Carefully, she scanned each green stripe, following it from the place it entered the scene until it merged with a larger stripe. One of the green bands stopped abruptly halfway to the horizon; it skirted a plateau and cut through a mesa, then rolled across a wide plain to stop abruptly at the base of a rocky escarpment.

"That looks like as good as possibility as any," she told the now-tiring horse and turned his head in the direction of what she hoped was Lost River.

In the end, it was Champion rather than Gloriana that found the road construction camp. Night had fallen and the rangeland moved and echoed with the yelping of coyotes; the hooting of owls; and the secret, nighttime meanderings of shadowy half-figures that appeared briefly and then vanished in the dim light of a crescent moon. Gloriana drooped in the saddle, hanging onto the saddle horn, all attempts to guide her mount forgotten. Her legs felt numb, but sharp pains continued to pierce her side, and her shoulders ached dully. Champion had slowed to a walk, and his head, usually held high and proud, hung wearily; yet he kept on moving, his quick wits telling him that to stop alone in the open would mean certain death.

It was after midnight when they stumbled into Graham Norton's camp. Trembling, his sides flecked with foam, the horse stood quietly within the circle of firelight while eager hands took the burden from his back and relieved him of his saddle. Soon he was rubbed down and resting contentedly among his fellows, a measure of oats in his nosebag and sleep just minutes away from heavy eyelids.

"Take care of Champion," Gloriana managed to murmur when hot coffee and a warm fire had revived her. She opened her eyes to find Graham's anxious face only inches away. "Graham! Thank God," she whispered and, throwing her arms impulsively around the startled man's neck, she hid her face against his rough flannel shirt.

He held her tightly for a moment, seemingly oblivious to his men's curious looks, then began to question her gently, "What happened, Glory? What are you running from?"

The story of her day's adventure tumbled out then—the silent sunrise, Oweena's warning, the men in the Indian costumes, her recognition of John Tilton, her escape and long ride, and the sounds and smoke of battle. She was crying when she finished, and the men looked grim but not surprised.

"I blame myself," Graham muttered hoarsely, the roughness of his voice betraying his emotion. "I should never have left them unprotected."

"You couldn't have known, boss," reassured one of the men Gloriana recognized as an old friend from her first trail ride.

"I don't think he would have come if he hadn't found my drawings," Gloriana added, and then she had to explain what had happened with the sketches in her journal and her last meeting with Tilton that ended in threats.

"It sounds like it's her he's after," Blackjack commented to Graham, who glared fiercely but said nothing.

"And that there means he'll be a-comin' for her jest as soon as he picks up her trail," Smitty agreed.

The certainty in the Westerners' voices awoke Gloriana to a possibility she had not considered. Somehow she had thought if she could just reach Graham, she would be safe, and he would be able to send back help to the mission. Now she realized that there were only a dozen men around the fire, and a wave of fear dampened her happiness.

"I'm afraid I have put you all in danger," she faltered.

"Don't be silly, Gloriana," Graham told her impatiently. He gave her a little shake but did not take his arm from around her shoulders.

"Whatever we are going to do will have to wait until morning," he said. "Tilton won't travel at night, and there is always the chance that some of the Klamaths will be keeping him busy." He posted a

194

watch and told the others to get some sleep, but he himself continued to sit beside Gloriana, looking gloomily into the night.

Now was the time to resolve their differences, but Gloriana had no idea where to begin. In the firelight Graham's face seemed distant and closed, and though he still held her, he did not appear to be aware of the fact.

She would have preferred for him to make the first move, but it did not look like he was going to do so. With a sigh she let her arm, which had slipped from around his neck, encircle his waist, and she snuggled against him. The action brought an immediate response. He squeezed her closely, but his expression was troubled.

"I'm sorry I allowed you to be exposed to this danger," he told her finally. "I knew Tilton was not to be trusted."

"I should have figured it out myself," Gloriana blamed herself. Then she took a deep breath and added, "I guess I was so busy fighting with you that I couldn't think straight about anything else."

Graham lifted her head from his shoulder with his free hand so that he could look into her eyes. His gaze was searching and his voice serious. "Does that mean that we are through fighting?"

"I don't ever want to fight with you again." She did not wait for his response but lifted her lips to his and kissed him shyly at first and then hungrily. Graham's reaction was everything she could have wished.

After a breathless moment in which she wondered if her ribs were being crushed, he began to explain, "Glory, I want you to know that girl never meant anything to me."

"I know; she told me," Gloriana responded before she thought.

She felt him stiffen, and then he asked somewhat tensely, "Would you have believed me if she hadn't told you?"

But Gloriana would not allow him to move away or be offended. She had had enough of misunderstandings to last a lifetime, so she kissed the hard outline of his jaw and then let her lips travel softly over his neck.

Graham laughed delightedly in spite of himself. "I don't know what happened to my blushing Philadelphia lady, but I like it," he whispered against her hair.

"It's simple. I discovered I couldn't live without you. After that it was easy to see what a fool I had been not to have trusted you all along. I should have known when you accepted Christ as your Saviour, that you were not the kind of man I was accusing you of being, and I think I did know. I was just too proud to admit it."

CHAPTER 20

GLORIANA WOKE THE NEXT MORNING to find herself at
the base of the rocky escarpment that she had seen
the day before looking out over the rangeland. Nearby
was a straggling wood made up primarily of junipers,
scrub oaks, and lodgepole pines, and a few yards
away a wide, shallow river—its color nearly gray
from a bed of slate and pebbles and a border of sage—
disappeared into the ground.

"Lost River," she recognized it and looked around
for the magnificent animal who had brought her there.
She saw him in a rope corral, his nose once again in a
feedbag, and hobbled over to tell him good morning.
The stitch in her side was gone, but the charley horses
in her legs were not, and every muscle in her body felt
as though it had been stretched and pummeled.

"You seem to have survived our adventure better
than I." Champion responded with a playful nudge
that nearly sent her sprawling, then went on eating.
He seemed none the worse for wear. His dark red
coat had been rubbed free of dust, and a night's rest
had made him eager to go again. "I'm afraid I don't

have either your stamina or your spirit," she told him with a playful tug on his forelock. How could such a noble beast belong to such an ignoble man?

"Isn't that John Tilton's horse?" Graham asked, joining her with a low whistle as he recognized the animal.

Gloriana nodded and then explained how she had gotten the horse.

"Who would have thought that the little Quaker missionary would become a frontier heroine!" Graham laughed, but his look was genuinely admiring. "You'll have some wonderful stories to tell our children," he added softly, and Gloriana found she was blushing with both embarrassment and pleasure.

She found a secluded place in the wood near the river to make her morning preparations. She was glad she had had the foresight to bring a change of clothing. The heavy shirt she had worn the day before clung to her skin as though she had worn it a week, but washing in the river's cool waters and donning a lighter blouse refreshed her. She combed her hair out of its long braids and tied it back with a ribbon. She could not see her face, but her cheeks and nose stung, and she tried not to imagine how she would look with a red, peeling sunburn.

"Miss Glory, Graham said you were to eat all of this," the cook told her with a grin when she returned to camp. Gloriana looked with dismay at the heaped-up sourdough biscuits, fried meat, and potatoes, but, digging in, she found to her amazement that she was hungry enough to devour nearly all of it. She noticed then that the men were breaking camp. Mules were being hitched to wagons loaded with equipment. The horses that were not saddled were being herded into a tight remuda to be driven along with the wagons.

"I'm going to put you up on Champion again," Graham told her as he hurried past. "He's strong enough to run away from anything if there's trouble, and I doubt Tilton has any other animals with his speed." To Gloriana's unspoken question, he replied. "He should have picked up your trail by now, but we'll have quite a few hours' start by the time he finds this camp."

Such, however, was not the case.

A lookout posted atop the escarpment halloaed the camp and called out, "Riders coming!" He had spotted a moving dust cloud coming fast from the east.

"He didn't bother to track you through the forest," Graham, suddenly understanding, explained to Gloriana. "He guessed where you would be heading and took the easier route along the east side of the lake."

Graham had planned to take the wagons and travel west, hoping to meet the larger part of his workcrew. They should have left Applegate Landing several days before with a party of surveyors and additional wagonloads of equipment. He had gambled on meeting them at Annie Creek, this side of the Greensprings, but that was a chance he could no longer take.

"We could hold them off in one of those caves down in the Lava Beds," one of the men suggested, pointing toward the black, ragged fields of once molten rock on the southern horizon.

"They could keep us there for weeks, starve us out, and no one would ever know what happened," Graham rejected the idea. "No, we'll have to split up. Gloriana and I will make tracks for Fort Winnemucca while the rest of you try to find our work gang and head north to the mission. If anyone's left alive, they'll need help."

The men objected to the plan. Gloriana caught their hint that she would slow their progress, but she could not dispute it. Her journey the day before had been leisurely compared to the pace they would have to set today, and already her aching body felt played out. She dreaded getting into the saddle and she feared the return of the pain in her side that she knew Champion's gallop would bring. But most of all, Graham's words, "if anyone's left alive," echoed through her mind, leaving her with an empty place at the center of her being, where hope had dwelt.

"It looks like about thirty or forty riders," the lookout, who had scrambled down the cliff face, reported to Graham. "They should be here in about an hour, maybe less."

Then everyone was moving. Horses whinnied, mules brayed, and wheels groaned as the wagons got underway. And heading in the opposite direction were Gloriana Windemere and Graham Norton.

"They'll have traveled all night while we've rested," Graham told Gloriana encouragingly, but both knew that it would take a miracle to save them; both were looking for that miracle to the only Source that could grant it. Through Graham's mind raced the outlaw's threats against Gloriana, and he pleaded on her behalf, while Gloriana thought of Tilton's jealous anger and the revenge he would take, as she prayed for Graham's safety.

The horses ran easily, covering ground at a good pace. Graham's buckskin, a solidly built animal with a deep chest and long back legs that evidenced a hint of Arabian blood, was slower than Champion, but his staying power was as great. The ground which looked flat from a distance proved treacherous close at hand. Rain-washed gullies crisscrossed, while prairie-dog towns mined the turf and sandy soil with holes—any of which could break a horse's leg or send a rider sprawling.

To Gloriana's inexperienced eyes, every direction looked the same. There were no landmarks, no trails to go by. Miles and miles of gray-green hills and mesas stretched to dim horizons. Graham worried about the trail they were leaving although Gloriana could see no trace of hoofprints behind them.

200

"We'll cover our tracks in Tule Lake," he said and pointed toward a misty haze to the south that looked more like a desert waste than a lake.

They had topped a rise when they heard the sounds of gunshots behind them. The long reports of rifles mixed with the shorter reports of pistol fire in a ragged staccato.

"What's happening? Did Tilton follow your crew after all?" Gloriana turned to Graham inquiringly.

The big man shook his head firmly. "My guess is the men set up a rear guard to give us a better chance to escape." He went to his saddlebags and took out a looking glass and used it to scan the horizon.

"John Tilton has one of those," Gloriana remembered.

"Then he's probably using it on us right now," Graham growled, angry with himself for exposing their position. He directed Gloriana to take the horses behind a nearby outcropping of rock and continued to peer through the glass.

What he saw made his tightly set lips press in an even tighter seam. "It didn't work," he told Gloriana briefly. "Tilton left half his men to fight. He and the rest are coming after us."

The chase continued mile after mile. Graham used every trick he knew, starting false trails down gullies and across rocky mesas. For a half hour they walked their horses in the edge of Tule Lake—a vast, shallow plain of water and reeds, more like a dense marsh than a lake. But when they emerged from the screens of cattails and bushes, Tilton and his men were still behind them, closer then before.

"They're running their horses into the ground," Graham commented. Their pursuers were close enough now that they could make out the figures of individual riders in the dust cloud behind them. In the forefront, his anger almost discernible even at that great distance, was John Tilton. "I'm going to hit the

Winnemucca Trail and try to outrun them," Graham told her. "Champion still has a burst of speed in him. When I give the signal, dig your heels into his sides and don't look back."

"I'm not leaving you," Gloriana shot back defiantly, but there was no time to argue.

The Winnemucca Trail was little more than a pair of wagon ruts cutting through the sand, rocks, and grass, but it was free of prairie-dog holes and other obstructions. Given their heads, Champion and Graham's buckskin lengthened their strides drawing upon some inner strength. They had begun to increase their lead, drawing away from the exhausted horses of the pursuers when a single rifle shot rang out.

Graham reeled in his saddle, and the buckskin broke stride. Gloriana pulled frantically on Champion's reins, but Graham shouted "Keep going!" One arm hung limp at his side, but with the other he was pulling his rifle from its sheath by his stirrup.

"I won't leave you!" Gloriana shouted back. Tears were streaming down her face as she tried to turn her plunging mount. The reins cut into her gloved hands, while Champion, frightened by the gunshot and her terror, fought her for the bit.

She heard the pounding of hoofs behind her and the wild shouts of Tilton and his men. Then she became confused as the pounding seemed to be coming from in front of her as well. "Gloriana Windemere, don't you dare lose consciousness!" she yelled at herself, and finally she had Champion turned and running back toward the place where Graham sat, shooting from the back of his trembling horse.

"Wherever thou goest, I will go," she said aloud, though there was no chance of his hearing her in the noise. Still he glanced over his shoulder as she rode up, but his anguished expression soon turned to bewilderment. With twenty outlaws shooting at him, a bullet hole in his shoulder, and the rifle in his hand hot and jammed, Graham Norton broke into a wide grin. For behind Gloriana at full gallop came a troop of soldiers from Fort Winnemucca. They had spread out in attack formation while a bugler sounded the charge. The officer at their head was waving a curved, silver saber that glistened menacingly in the sun and beside him, on a brown and white spotted pony, raced Chief Keintepoos. His shrill war whoop pierced through the din, a sound so savage and fierce as to numb the hearts of his enemies, but it made Gloriana's leap with thankfulness.

"It looks like Someone does care about us," she told Graham, though she doubted he could hear her.

Still he must have read her lips because he answered, "I know He does."

Rounding up the phony renegades did not take long. The men were too bewildered to put up much of a fight, and the horses were too tired to run. Somehow in the confusion John Tilton managed to escape. His horse was found ridden to death near Tule Lake, but though they searched the ground along the shore for miles, looking for his tracks, there was no sign of the outlaw.

"He will probably head south to San Francisco and, if he makes it past the Shasta Indians, he may find a new gang of cut throats on the Barbary Coast." Graham's prediction sounded gloomy, but it was merely a matter of fact. For now with his wound tended and Gloriana close by, he was contented.

The officer in charge of the cavalry troop was Major William F. Creighton, a middle-aged man whose years of service on the frontier were emblazoned in his insignia and evidenced by the calm efficiency of his actions. He dispatched some of his men to relieve Graham's work crew back at Lost River; the rest he set to making camp and treating the wounds of outlaws, soldiers, and animals alike.

"Well, it seems you have had some excitement,

Miss Windemere," Major Creighton began with a kindly smile that seemed to say it was all in a day's work for him. His bearded face and his manner were almost fatherly, and Gloriana found herself telling him about the escape from the mission, the ride south, and their pursuit by Tilton's outlaws. The officer nodded understandingly, but his face betrayed no surprise or astonishment.

"When this West is finally settled, I wonder how many people will realize what it took to tame her," he said musingly after she had finished.

"And I wonder how many will realize that it was often our own white savages, not the Indians, who needed taming," Graham interposed. "But tell us, Major, who is John Tilton and how did you know we needed help?"

Major Creighton looked sad then and his eyes assumed a faraway look. "John Tilton was the son of an old friend of mine—a promising young officer of sterling qualities. He was noted for his bright green eyes and his almost silver-white hair." The Major paused to note their reactions, then continued, "He was dispatched into Klamath territory to make peace with Chief Keintepoos and Chief John. We suspect now that he and all of his troopers were killed—ambushed perhaps by the man who assumed his identity."

"Then who is the man we have been calling John Tilton?" Gloriana asked with a little shudder as she recalled the months she had been in close contact with such a cold-blooded murderer.

"We think he may be a cavalry captain who was drummed out of the service a couple of years ago in Arizona."

"I heard one of his men call him Captain once," Gloriana remembered.

The Major nodded again, but he would say no more about the identity of the outlaw. Instead he turned to

204

their other question. "As for our being here at the right time and place, you can thank God and Keintepoos. The chief showed up at the fort two weeks ago with his story about phony soldiers masquerading as renegades."

"What made you believe him?" Graham asked. "You could have thought of him as an enemy."

"Since I knew the real John Tilton, his description of a dark-haired lieutenant was enough to make me suspicious. But what really turned the trick was he told me he was a Christian. You see, I am also a Christian, which made us brothers, and I had no choice but to believe a brother in Christ."

Late that night the soldiers returned, leading Graham's work crew and more prisoners. The men were sheepish as Graham chewed them out for disobeying his orders. But Smitty grinned slyly at Gloriana and said, "That's just the boss's way of sayin' thanks and he's glad we made it through all right."

Sometime between midnight and daybreak, a Klamath messenger found them in their lakeshore camp. Gloriana, sleeping on an army bedroll just inside the circle of firelight, heard the soft beats of the Indian pony's hooves, echoing through the ground. She sat up quickly, her heart beating faster before she remembered she was safe in an army camp and the man she had known as John Tilton had been defeated. She drifted back into a light sleep only to be awakened a few minutes later by a strong hand on her shoulder.

"It's a runner from the mission," Graham whispered, and in a second she was wide awake.

"Are they all right? Is anyone hurt?" She began asking questions, but he told her to wait. Keintepoos was questioning the messenger while the army major and some of his men looked on. The young brave had no wounds, but his scratched and dusty body showed evidence of a long, hard ride. The rapid speech was difficult to follow, but Gloriana could make out enough to breathe sighs of relief and prayers of thankfulness.

When she had escaped from the mission, she had gone with the feeling that their Klamath friends had deserted them. She understood now what Oweena had been trying to tell them that morning. The Klamaths had thought the attackers were after Indians, not missionaries, and they had withdrawn to a safe place protected by the warriors of Chief Keintepoos and Chief John. But when Oweena had recognized the lieutenant in his war paint and disguise, she had understood who the outlaws were really after and had ridden for help.

"Our people were not in time to save the buildings," Keintepoos told her regretfully, "but the missionaries are safe."

She knew a moment's regret for the picturesque quadrangle around the willow wood, the snug cabins, and the frontier hospital, but regrets were soon swallowed up in the joy of knowing that her uncle, Tildy, and the Midfields had survived.

But the tale had not ended happily for everyone. Before they attacked the mission, the outlaws had massacred a party of pioneers heading north with their loaded wagons.

"The Welshes," Gloriana guessed. "Bridgette knew too much, and she threatened to expose him." She remembered their suspicions that Welsh might be the leader of the renegades and wondered again how they could have been so blind. She could not be sorry that the elder Welsh would not be setting up his trading post to sell firewater to the Indians. But she was sorry for the mousy little mother, who tried so hard to please, and the happy-go-lucky boys who could have grown up to be fine men. And most of all she was sorry about Bridgette. *Perhaps if I had not been so jealous, perhaps if I had tried just a little bit, I could have been a good influence on her,* Gloriana thought with the wisdom of hindsight.

Then she noticed that the messenger was pointing at her and speaking in a low voice to Keintepoos. The warrior's strong face remained impassive, but humor lurked in his eyes as he approached her.

"He brings also a message from Chief John. The Chief has heard of your courage in escaping from the mission. He is raising his offer for you to a hundred ponies and two hundred beaver pelts."

CHAPTER 21

ON A GOLDEN JULY MORNING Gloriana Windemere awoke in a rainbow-tinted bedroom in Applegate Landing. Outside the open window, meadowlarks greeted the dawn while inside sunbeams danced across the flowered carpet. The music and beauty blended with the joy in her heart to make her feel like singing, for today was Gloriana's wedding day.

In the corner of the tiny room beside the prayer altar and rocking chair hung an old-fashioned wedding dress. A creamy confection of lace and silk, it had been Cynthia Applegate's own, and she had lovingly adapted it to Gloriana's taller, fuller figure. A high neck trimmed with lace topped a yoke neckline made demure by a gauze insert that would allow a glimpse without baring the delicate skin beneath. Long, tight sleeves of Brussels lace began in tiny puffs at the shoulders and ended in graceful V's above the fingers to give an appearance of gloves without covering the all-important ring finger. Seed pearls outlined the bodice and waist, dropping the latter slightly to emphasize its smallness. And the skirt was yards and yards of shimmering silk that peeked out from a half skirt of lace. Molded to the bride's form, it fell nearly straight in front, then swept back for an elegant train. A large white bow, fastened above the gathers and ending in wide streamers emphasized the bustle effect while a long veil cascading from a pearl-crusted crown trailed behind.

"I'll look like a living version of Bridal Veil Falls," Gloriana laughed delightedly as she remembered the lacy extravagance of the waterfall. At the same time she remembered the outlaw who had called himself John Tilton, and she breathed a deep prayer of thankfulness to her Heavenly Father who had made this day and her happiness possible.

She and the other missionaries had been at Applegate Landing for nearly a month. The hospitable Applegates had opened their home to Dr. Windemere's household, while the Reverend Samuels and his wife housed the Midfields. The old doctor had at first protested this sabbatical. He had wanted to stay on the Upper Klamath while Graham Norton and his men rebuilt the mission. But the bullet in his leg reduced his walk to a hobble, and the congestion in his lungs from having breathed too much smoke in the fires slowed his pace further. He had had to admit that he might be less than a help.

The Midfields would not be returning with him to work among the Klamaths. Dr. Midfield had been embarrassed and apologetic about their going home, but his wife had remained adamant. "I won't have my babies die in this wilderness," Catherine Midfield had said again and again. No one could assure her that they would not. The hardships and tragedies were as much a fact of frontier life as the glorious scenery.

Moreover, Dr. Windemere was losing Gloriana. After the wedding day her home would be in Applegate Landing where Graham had built a cabin as picturesque as the forest and where he could continue hauling freight from the coast.

"Well, Tildy, it looks like it's just you and me again," the doctor had told his housekeeper with an attempt to be cheerful about it. Then letters had come from the Mission Board at home. They had just heard about the numbers treated at the mission during the epidemic and also the rapport that had been established with the local tribes. They were dispatching a team of three doctors and four nurses and sending funds for the building and stocking of a large new hospital.

With his cup full Dr. Windemere could enjoy his niece's happiness and give her his blessing. There had, however, been one codicil to the Mission Board's decision:

> You have on your staff a single female nurse named Miss Gloriana Windemere. The Executive Committee of the Board has reviewed its policy concerning the employment of spinsters in the frontier settlements and has decided that the Subcommittee on Appointments exceeded its authority in granting her sponsorship. We are, therefore, requesting that her work with the mission be terminated and she be returned home. The board will defray all expenses if she embarks on the return journey by mid-August.

Dr. Windemere had been bemused by the order, but Gloriana had been incensed. She had demanded that her uncle write a letter of protest, and she had herself composed a scathing attack on the Board's reasoning, its competence, and its knowledge of frontier conditions. He had more or less agreed but vaguely enough to suggest that he might put off the task indefinitely. "After all, you are leaving the mmssion anyway," he had reminded her.

And she was. During the past weeks while Graham was back at Klamath Mission, she had been turning his cabin into a home. A large, spacious building of unpeeled logs, it sat on the edge of the settlement on a bluff overlooking the Rogue River. At its back were giant trees, and before it lay the rolling green valley, stretching away to the white-topped peaks of the Cascade Range.

In her room at the Applegate's, Gloriana settled into a rocker and, reaching for her journal, began to thumb through the pages. How glad she was that she had taken it with her when she escaped from the mission. Otherwise, it would have been burned with the rest of her possessions.

She had come far in just one year. Some of her ideas and attitudes had changed, but mostly they had grown, shedding the veneer of sophistication and getting down to the homely truths that gave the pioneers something to hang onto through the trials and hardships of frontier life. She now understood that they were an intelligent, cultured people who needed her God, not her social rules. And no longer was freedom frightening to her, but an opportunity to create a new and better way of life where all of God's people could work together in harmony and kinship.

With a little half-smile on her lips, Gloriana picked up her pencil and began writing her wedding day entry—the last one as Miss Gloriana Windemere of Philadelphia.

Applegate Landing   July 16, 1852
My Wedding Day

Today I stop being a spinster nurse from Philadelphia and become Mrs. Graham Norton of Applegate Landing. Back home the marriage of the elder Miss Windemere, daughter of the Reverend Windemere of Seventh Avenue Church, would have been no more than a minor ripple in the social whirlpool, but here on the frontier it is a major event. For two days now the guests have been coming— pioneers from as far away as the Umpqua Valley, miners from the gold fields at Jacksonville, and Klamath and Shasta friends from their distant summer camps in the Cascade Mountains.

I suppose I should be sad not to have my sisters Juliana and Marianna with me at such an important time, and part

211

of me does miss them. But my matron of honor will be Princess Oweena, wife of Chief Keintepoos. Keintepoos will stand up with Graham. Some people in the village have thought our choice odd and even inappropriate, but we are happy with our decision. These people are among our closest friends. We have gone through fire and water together, and now that we are in a happy place, we want them to share it with us.

I asked Oweena and Keintepoos to wear their own wedding garments for the ceremony. Made of soft white deerskin, fringed, and decorated in intricate designs of beads and dyed porcupine quills—they are as exquisite in their own way as the elegant gown of lace and silk that I am to wear.

Brides are supposed to be nervous, but I feel only a great joy welling up from somewhere deep inside me. Perhaps that is because I have no reservations about my marriage. I know it is what God wants for me, and I know too that the love Graham and I have for each other is rooted in our deeper love for Him.

The years ahead will not all be rosy. I have seen enough now of the Oregon Territory to know that living here will not be like setting up housekeeping on a peaceful boulevard back home. Many of the Indians are our friends, but there are some, I know, who look on us as enemies. Outlaws like the man we knew as John Tilton are still at large. And it will be many years before the quality of medical care will be comparable to that in the East.

Still I would not trade the life I have begun here for a New York mansion or a princess's palace. This is where I belong—in the center of God's will. Here in Applegate Landing I will raise my children, dedicate them to God and teach them to be strong men and women. And here I will do my best to make this wonderful Oregon Territory, the Land of the Golden West, a place where Christian men and women of all races can work together for a better life for everyone.

The sun was setting when Gloriana glided regally down a grassy aisle to meet her groom. In her hand she carried a bouquet of creamy white mountain lilies and delicate maidenhair fern. Her slippered feet trod on the pink and yellow petals of wild roses, and the air was perfumed with wildflowers, pine, and cedar. Around her neck was a tiny mother-of-pearl cross, a gift from the groom and the "something new" demanded by custom. Her beautiful ruby engagement ring was "something old," since it had been a legacy to Graham from his grandmother who had been given it upon her own engagement nearly a century before. The "something borrowed" was her wedding gown, and for "something blue"—Gloriana blushed at the thought of the lacey blue garter that she wore carefully hidden beneath layers of skirt and petticoat. It had been a gift from Rita, the saloon girl turned pioneer wife and church pianist. She had married the compassionate young miner who had sympathized when her arm was broken on the trip from Crescent City.

Graham Norton, watching Gloriana float gracefully toward him, saw the blush and wondered what had embarrassed his beautiful bride. Perhaps it had been the intensity of his expression or the unaccustomed situation of being the cynosure of so many eyes.

The color of Graham's dark suit accentuated his height, while the severe cut emphasized his broad shoulders. His hair had been newly trimmed and vigorously brushed to approximate some order, yet the red-gold curls were beginning to spring above his ears and trail across his wide forehead.

"Chief John would give two, maybe three, hundred horses if he could see her now," Keintepoos, who stood closely beside Graham, told him quietly. The warrior's expression was impassive, but Graham was beginning to understand the man's understated humor.

"Not for a thousand," Graham whispered back.

Gloriana wondered if they were talking about her, but she caught the mischievous glint in the chief's glance and guessed it was some joke. She had to catch her breath when she looked at Graham. Never had he seemed more handsome or more awesomely masculine. Her uncle, who guided her toward the altar, caught the little gasp and patted her hand reassuringly. He had chosen to give her away rather than perform the ceremony himself—"My big chance to play Papa," the old bachelor had said—and it was silver-haired Reverend Samuels of Applegate Landing who waited beside Graham. On each side of the aisle were what seemed like masses of people—a sea of bobbing heads as the guests tried to get a better look at the bride.

The altar had been laid at the base of a magnificent stand of pines. Like green spires the noble trees pointed heavenward. From behind them a setting sun sent golden rays through the branches and lighted the western sky, visible between the green arches, like a cathedral's stained glass windows.

"How glorious!" she murmured as Graham reached for her hand.

His reply was a rapt yes, but he was looking at Gloriana instead of the sunset.

Reverend Samuels smiled benevolently as the bride and groom joined hands. With his nimbus of white hair he looked like some angel sent from heaven, and his voice held an unearthly sweetness when he began speaking the old and precious words.

"Dearly beloved, we are gathered today in the sight of God and man to join this man and this woman in holy matrimony."

Gloriana and Graham turned to each other with the glow of the setting sun on their faces. In their eyes, as in their hearts, was a holy love, and the vows they exchanged were pure and tried, like the gold in the rings that bound them together.